PREGNANT MISTRESSES

*She's having his baby—
but she longs for his love...*

She's been seduced in the bedroom, and now
she's pregnant by the man of her dreams.
But will she ever have the one thing she wants
more than anything—his love?

Don't miss any of the stories this month in
Modern Love!

HEIDI RICE was born and bred—and still lives—in London, England. She has two boys who love to bicker, a wonderful husband who, luckily for everyone, has loads of patience, and a supportive and ever-growing British/French/Irish/American family. As much as Heidi adores the "Big Smoke," she also loves America, and every two years or so she and her best friend leave hubby and kids behind and *Thelma and Louise* it across the States for a couple of weeks (although they always leave out the driving-off-a-cliff bit). She's been a film buff since her early teens, and a romance junkie for almost as long. She's indulged her first love by being a film reviewer for the past ten years. Then two years ago she decided to spice up her life by writing romance. Discovering the fantastic sisterhood of romance writers (both published and unpublished) in Britain and America made it a wild and wonderful journey to her first Harlequin novel, and she's looking forward to many more to come. Heidi loves to hear from her readers. Contact her by visiting her Web site on www.heidi-rice.com or e-mailing her at heidi@heidi-rice.com.

Heidi Rice

Bedded by a Playboy

HARLEQUIN®

TORONTO • NEW YORK • LONDON
AMSTERDAM • PARIS • SYDNEY • HAMBURG
STOCKHOLM • ATHENS • TOKYO • MILAN • MADRID
PRAGUE • WARSAW • BUDAPEST • AUCKLAND

ISBN-13: 978-0-373-82087-0
ISBN-10:   0-373-82087-9

BEDDED BY A PLAYBOY

Previously published in the U.K. under the title
BEDDED BY THE BAD BOY.

First North American Publication 2008.

www.eHarlequin.com

Printed in U.S.A.

Bedded by a Playboy

To my best mate, Catri, for all those Navajo frybread moments. May we have many more. And to my husband, Rob, for helping make my dream come true.

I hope yours does, too.

CHAPTER ONE

'WHOEVER he is, he's completely naked,' Jessie Connor said as quietly as possible. Not easy with the heat flaring in her cheeks and her heartbeat pounding like a sledgehammer in her ears.

The most magnificent male specimen she had ever seen stood less than fifteen yards away. Stark naked. Thank goodness, he had his back to her, or her heart would have stopped beating altogether.

Dark tangles of wet hair flowed down to touch broad shoulders. Roped with muscle, his bronzed skin glistened in the afternoon sunlight as water dripped off his powerful physique and onto the white stone tiles of the pool patio. Oh, my.

Jessie edged back. She could feel the warm, weathered wood of her sister Ali's Long Island home through the thin cotton of her blue sundress, but it was nothing compared to the heat throbbing low in her belly.

'Who is he? Do you recognise him?' Ali hissed next to her ear.

Jessie stared at her sister, huddled beside her behind the house. She took in Ali's worried frown and her round figure, distended in pregnancy. 'Well, I can't be absolutely positive from this angle, but I don't think I know him.'

'Move over, I'm taking a look.' Elbowing Jessie aside, Ali peered round the corner. After getting what Jessie considered more than a necessary eyeful for a married woman, Ali shuffled back. Her face had turned a vivid shade of scarlet. 'Wow, that bum's almost as gorgeous as Linc's.'

Jessie decided to ignore Ali's extremely inappropriate comment about her husband. 'Yes, but did you recognise it?'

'Of course not, I'm a married woman.'

'Now she remembers,' Jessie muttered.

'We've got to get out of here and call Linc.'

'Don't be daft. We can tackle him ourselves.'

Ali's eyebrows shot up. 'We most certainly cannot. I'm nearly eight months pregnant and he's enormous. Did you see those shoulders?'

'Yes, I did. Among other things.'

'You can't go out there. This is America. He could have a gun.'

'I'd like to know where he's got that hidden,' Jessie replied, her indignation rising. 'He's trespassing and I intend to tell him so. How dare he just come in and use the pool as if he owned the place?' Jessie glanced down at her sister's rounded belly. 'You better stay here.' She looked at her watch. 'Linc's due back with Emmy any minute.'

'What if he attacks you?' Ali's furious whisper sounded desperate.

'Don't worry, I've got a plan.'

Ali's brows set in a grim line. 'I don't think I want to hear this.'

'It worked a treat for Bruce Willis in *Die Hard 2.*'

'Oh, for goodness' sake!'

'Shh.' Jessie pressed a finger to her lips. 'He may be built but he's probably not deaf.' Taking a steadying breath, she leaned back around the corner and took another peek at their trespasser.

Jessie's teeth tugged on her bottom lip. Ali was probably right. They shouldn't approach him. But ever since they had returned from her sister's hospital appointment and spotted the powerful black motorcycle sitting in the driveway, the sizzle of adrenaline had been surging through Jessie's veins.

Impulsiveness was her worse trait. Hadn't Toby, her stuffy ex-fiancé, told her as much the whole two years they'd been going out? 'If only you were as reckless in bed as you are out of it,' he'd shouted at her during their final titanic row six months ago.

Jessie squinted as the sun sparkled off the surface of the pool. She watched as the stranger towelled himself dry with an old T-shirt. The familiar anger at Toby's insults flashed through her. Well, Toby could take his opinion and shove it in a place where the sun didn't shine. She wasn't reckless—or frigid, for that matter—it had just taken her a while to realise that Toby Collins wasn't the Mr Right she'd spent her whole life looking for. He hadn't needed her the way she'd thought he had. While she'd been dreaming of making a home, having children, building a family together, Toby had been fantasising about having a wildcat in bed and a mouse out of it. It still infuriated her that it had taken her two long years to figure it out.

The trespasser pulled a pair of jeans over his long legs. Jessie ignored the quick stab of disappointment as his beautiful bum disappeared behind faded denim.

Men! Jessie clenched her teeth. She simply was not going to let this arrogant stranger get away with his outrageous behaviour.

She toed off her sandals, her mind made up. 'Right, I'm off,' she whispered to Ali. 'You better go back to the car and call Linc.'

'Don't… Jess…'

Neatly sidestepping her sister's grabbing fingers, Jessie crept out from behind the safety of the building. Time to teach their trespasser a lesson.

Monroe Latimer fastened the threadbare jeans and stuck his hands into the pockets to straighten them. The tips of his fingers touched the old letter he'd been carrying around for over a year. He pulled out the heavily creased envelope. A drop of water slapped onto the paper, smudging the Key West address of his old parole officer, Jerry Myers. He raked the dripping hair off his forehead. Sighing, he wondered for about the hundredth time what had made him keep the damn thing for so long. And what had possessed him to take that exit off the interstate when he'd spotted the sign to the Hamptons this morning.

Curiosity. Monroe shook his head—just the sort of impulse he was usually smart enough to avoid. He pulled the letter out of its envelope and scanned the contents, though he knew them by heart.

Dear Monroe,
   You don't know me, but my name's Alison Latimer and I'm your sister-in-law. I'm married to your older brother Lincoln. Linc's been trying to track you down for a long

time now. I'm sending this letter to Jerry Myers, in the hope he will pass it on to you.

Linc and I have been married for five years. We're based in London, but we spend July to September every year in our summer house on Oceanside Drive, East Hampton, Long Island.

Please, Monroe, come and visit us. Linc and I would love you to stay for a while. From what Jerry tells me, Linc's the only family you have left. I know you haven't seen Linc in over twenty years, but he never stopped looking for you.

Family is important, Monroe.

Please come. Love Ali

Good thing the first line of the return address had been rubbed off the back of the letter months ago. He might have been dumb enough to go knocking on his brother's door, if he'd had the right house number. Of course, the minute he got to Oceanside Drive, he knew he shouldn't have come. Guys like him only came to neighbourhoods like this one if they were doing yard work.

Monroe crumpled up the letter, shoved it back in his pocket. At least now he could throw it away. He'd seen the way his brother and sister-in-law lived. No way was he ever going to follow up on their invitation. He didn't belong here. He had his Harley, his battered box of oil paints, spare clothes and a bedroll, and he had himself. That was all he needed; that was all he was ever going to need.

Alison Latimer was wrong. Family wasn't important. Not to him. He'd been free to do what he pleased, when he pleased, for the last fourteen years and that was the way he intended to keep it. Family was just another kind of prison and he'd had enough of that to last him a lifetime.

He pushed away the familiar bitterness. He could hear the rustle of a sea breeze through the flowerbed by the pool. Angling his head, he caught the fresh perfume of sweet summer blooms mixed with the chemical scent of chlorine—and grinned. Well, hell, at least he'd gotten a swim in a ritzy pool in one of the most beautiful homes he'd ever seen.

He'd been turning the Harley around, ready to head back to the interstate, when his artist's eye had spotted the wood and glass structure rising out of the sand dunes. Situated on its own at the end of the chunk of land that jutted out into the Atlantic Ocean, the modern structure had seemed to beckon him. Like all the other houses in the area, the grounds were surrounded by deer fencing and a high privet hedge, but Monroe had spotted the edge of the pool, winking at him in the sunlight as the bike had purred over the rise and down into the driveway. He'd been grimy and dog-tired, had been on the bike since daybreak in Maryland and he still had another few hours to go until he hit New York. The place was hidden from the road. He'd pressed the door buzzer to make sure no one was home and a quick check of the security system had told him it wasn't armed. So he'd boosted himself over the main gate and enjoyed the luxury of an afternoon swim. The thrill he recalled so well from his childhood of doing something forbidden on a lazy summer afternoon had been a nice fringe benefit.

Better hit the road now, though. The owners could return any minute and call the cops. With his record, it wouldn't go easy on him if he got caught trespassing. Time to move on.

Keeping her breathing slow and steady, Jessie tiptoed across the patio. She stopped dead when her trespasser shoved whatever it was he'd been staring at back into his pocket. When he didn't turn around, but reached for his T-shirt, she let go of the breath caught in her throat.

Humming some tuneless melody, he sat down on the sun-drenched tiles, rubbed his feet with the T-shirt and picked up a sock.

Sticking her two fingers out, Jessie shoved the points between his shoulder blades and shouted out in her most authoritative voice, 'Don't move. I have a gun.'

He stopped humming, his back went rigid and he dropped his sock.

'Okay, don't get excited.' His voice was gruff and tight with annoyance. He sounded American, but there was something else about his accent she couldn't quite place.

'Put your hands up, but don't turn around.'

His skin felt warm, but the muscles beneath were hard as rock, flexing under her fingers as he raised his arms. Up close, he looked a lot more dangerous. Jessie spotted a faded tattoo across his left bicep. Ridged white scar lines criss-crossed the tanned skin of his back. But then she noticed something else. Despite the impressive muscles across his shoulders and upper arms, he didn't have an ounce of fat on him. He was so lean, she could make out his ribs. A Goliath who didn't eat properly? How odd.

'Listen, put the gun down and I'll get out of here. No harm, no foul.'

He started to turn. She prodded her fingers harder into his spine. 'Don't turn around, I said.'

'Easy.' He didn't sound scared, just really pissed off. Maybe this hadn't been such a great idea after all. 'I'm putting my hands down,' he ground out. 'I've been on the bike all day and I'm beat.' He lowered his arms.

The seconds ticked by interminably.

'So what do we do now?' he asked.

Jessie's heart hammered against her rib-cage and sweat pooled between her breasts. Hell, she hadn't thought this far ahead. Where was Linc? Her fingers were starting to hurt.

'Where you from? You sound English?' he said.

'I think where you're from is probably a more pertinent question,' Jessie shot back. No arrogant trespasser was going to charm her.

He leaned forward. Jessie's heart jolted in her chest. 'What are you doing?'

'Grabbing my socks. Any objections?' The response was measured, calm and condescending.

Jessie bristled. 'Fine, but next time ask permission.' Just as she issued the order her tightly clamped fingers twitched.

The trespasser's back tensed and his head swung round. Oops! 'Damn it!'

Jessie jumped back, yelping, as her prey shot up and grabbed her in one quick, furious movement.

'Let me go,' she shrieked, struggling to pull her arms free as his large hands clamped on them like manacles.

'The finger routine. I got to hand it to you, I never thought I'd fall for that one.'

Striking blue eyes stared daggers at her out of a face that would have done Michelangelo proud. The man was quite simply beautiful. Jessie gulped, momentarily transfixed, taking in the high, slashing cheekbones, the rakish stubble on his chin and the dare-devil scar across his left eyebrow. Adonis or not, his face was as hard as granite. He looked ready to murder someone and, from the way his fingers dug into her arms, she knew exactly who it was.

Her heart rate shot up to warp speed. Don't pass out, you silly cow. This is no time to panic. Twisting, Jessie kicked out with her bare foot and connected with his shin.

'Ow! Stop that, you little...' he yelled, yanking her towards him and wrapping his arms around her.

'Let me go. You—you trespasser.' With her face pressed against the soft, curling hair on his chest, the demand came out on a muffled squeak. The smell of fresh, wet male was overpowering. She lifted her knee, intending to stamp on his foot, but before she could make contact he tensed and shot backwards.

'Watch out!'

His hands let go. Jessie turned, poised to bolt for freedom, but he grabbed her from behind. Strong arms banded under her breasts, he lifted her off the ground as if she weighed nothing at all. She kicked, frantically, but he was holding her so close, so tight, she couldn't get any leverage.

Okay, now was the perfect time to panic.

'My sister's in the house with a shotgun,' she squealed.

'Yeah, right.' His arms tightened, cutting off more of her air supply. 'You're a danger to society, you know that?'

The buzzing in Jessie's ears became deafening. She was going to faint. His whole body was wrapped around her. His size, his strength, overwhelmed her. Why hadn't she listened to Ali? How the hell did she always get into these situations? And how was she going to get out of this one?

The whisper of his breathing against her ear made her shudder.

What would Bruce do now? Think, woman, think. 'I'm warning you,' she said, through gritted teeth. 'If you don't let me go, I'll hurt you, a lot.'

Monroe's lips twitched. Having gotten over the humiliation of falling for his captive's harebrained stunt, he had to admire her gall. The threat was ridiculous. She was close to a foot shorter than him and slender, too, despite the impressive curves he could feel pressed against his forearms. 'You're a real firecracker, aren't you?'

She must have heard the admiration in his voice, because she went very still. He loosened his arms a little. He should probably let her go and get the hell out of here, but she felt good in his arms, round and soft in all the right places. He wasn't going to hurt her, but he figured she deserved a little payback. After all, she'd scared the hell out of him.

'So how exactly are you going to hurt me?' He purred the words in her ear.

'You don't frighten me, you complete sod.'

'Sod, huh?' He grinned; her clipped, precise accent made her sound like the lady of the manor addressing one of her peasants. It made him think of all those summers he'd spent in London as a kid with his English grandmother. It was one of the very few good memories from his childhood. He grinned. 'You are English, I'd know that accent anywhere. Hell, I'm half English myself. Kind of.'

'Isn't that flipping lovely for you?'

Funny, but she didn't remind him of prim and proper Granny Lacey one bit.

'Tut-tut.' He inhaled the heady scent from her wildly curling hair. 'And my sweet little granny always used to say English manners were the best in the world.'

'I'll give you manners,' she snarled, wriggling some more.

He laughed, really starting to enjoy himself. She was rigid in his arms, but he could feel her chest heaving with fury. He could imagine that pretty face of hers, glowing with temper. High cheekbones, smooth peach-toned skin, the sprinkle of freckles across her pert little nose, and those large, expressive sea-green eyes. He'd only glimpsed her face for a moment, but it had made a hell of an impression. She struggled again, and the firm swell of her butt pressed against his naked belly through the clingy little dress she had on.

The strong surge of arousal surprised him. He tightened his arms. She smelled good, too. 'You know, you're cute.' He smiled, nuzzling her hair. 'When you're not trying to kill me.'

'You are so going to die,' she snapped back.

'Get your hands off her!'

Monroe's head jerked up.

A man with a savage scowl on his face marched across the patio towards them. The little girl skipping along beside him didn't make him look any less threatening. Monroe registered the heavily pregnant woman behind them, but kept his gaze focused on the big guy.

The situation didn't seem quite so funny any more.

'Damn it.' Monroe let go of Miss Firecracker. She turned, glared at him, her green eyes sparking with fury, and then dashed over to the pregnant lady.

'Who are you and what the hell are you doing on my property?' the man bellowed.

Monroe held up his hands and tried to think fast. The guy was maybe an inch over his own six feet two and well built, but the tailored pants and pricey designer polo shirt he wore made him look rich and cultured. Monroe figured he could take him. But he couldn't swing at the guy when he had a kid beside him. And he didn't want to add assault to a trespassing charge if the cops arrived. Which left diplomacy as his only option.

'I just took a swim in your pool. I thought the place was empty.'

'Well, it's not.' The big guy ground the words out, his ice-blue eyes blazing with temper. 'Stay with Jessie, Emmy,' he said as he pushed the little girl behind him.

Monroe spotted Miss Firecracker take hold of the child's hand. The redhead was still glaring at him—and starting to look very self-satisfied.

The guy pushed the sleeves of his polo shirt up forearms that were ridged with muscle. 'I'm going to teach this idiot a lesson.'

A sick feeling in his gut, Monroe realised he'd have to take the punch. He closed his eyes, braced for the pain.

Then the pregnant lady shouted, 'Stop, Linc, stop!'

When nothing happened, Monroe risked opening one eye. The woman had a hold of the man's arm but she was staring right at him. 'Who are you?' she asked softly.

'Nobody, ma'am. All I took was a swim.' If only he could just deck the guy and get out of here.

'You're Monroe.' She said the words so quietly, Monroe wasn't sure he'd heard her right.

'What the hell is going on?' Mr Furious shouted back, still busting to take a swing at him.

'Linc, he's your brother. Can't you see the resemblance?'

Oh, hell. It hit Monroe just who these people were. He tried to swallow past the boulder in his throat, but his mouth had gone bone-dry. All he'd wanted was a quick swim and now look what he'd done.

'Monroe?' The big guy looked as if he'd taken a punch to the gut. Monroe knew how he felt.

He hadn't seen that face since he was ten years old, but now that he looked at it properly, Monroe recognised it all right. The guy had the same clear blue eyes as he did. And that mouth, that chin—didn't he see virtually the same ones in the mirror every time he remembered to shave?

'I should split,' Monroe mumbled.

Every one of them—his brother, the pregnant lady, who he figured must be his brother's wife, even the little girl and the woman with the flaming hair—was staring at him as if he'd grown two heads.

'I never thought I'd see you again.' His brother's voice was thready, his eyes shadowed.

'It's no big deal. It's a mistake. I shouldn't have used your pool.' Boy, was that the truth.

'I don't give a damn about the pool,' his brother said weakly.

'I need to go.' Monroe glanced at Miss Firecracker. She wasn't looking smug any more. Her face had gone stoplight-red to match that rioting hair.

His brother's wife stepped forward. 'You can't go, Monroe.' Her deep green eyes were steady on his. 'You and Linc have a lot of catching up to do. We want you to stay for a while. That's why we invited you.'

She seemed as if she meant it. Monroe felt honour-bound to set her straight. He didn't belong here; couldn't she see that? 'Look, ma'am, it's nice of you to ask me—' he huffed out a breath '—but I'm going to get on my way.'

He heard his brother curse, but his wife just shook her head, sadly. 'You're Linc's brother. You're family, Monroe. We want little Emily here to get to know you. You're her uncle.'

Monroe's gaze flicked to the little girl who was whispering furiously to Miss Firecracker and gazing at him in that penetrating way only kids could pull off.

He wasn't her uncle. He wasn't anyone's family.

'I'm Ali, by the way, Linc's wife,' the pregnant woman continued. 'That's our daughter Emmy and my sister Jessie.'

Monroe gave a stiff nod, the little girl waved back at him and said, 'Hi,' but the redhead just continued to stare at him. She didn't look anywhere near as welcoming as her sister.

'We've got five bedrooms in this place, Monroe,' his sister-in-law said as her fingers settled on his arm. 'Surely you can stay for a while and get to know us all.' The determination on her face told him there was no way she was going to let him bolt. The sinking sensation in his stomach dipped lower.

'I'm not staying in your home.' On that, he was firm.

'There's an apartment above the garage that will give you privacy.'

Monroe wondered if his sister-in-law had been a steamroller in a former life.

'Linc, why don't you take your brother into the house? Get him a beer, and then you can show him where he'll be staying.'

'Sure. Grab your stuff, Roe.'

The nickname reverberated in Monroe's mind, no one had called him that in close to twenty years.

'I think we both deserve a beer,' Linc said as he gave him a rueful smile. The crooked twist of his lips stabbed at Monroe's memory again.

'Hold on.' He hadn't agreed to anything, had he? But as he tried to form a protest, his sister-in-law picked up his T-shirt and shoved it on top of the boots in his arms.

'Hell,' Monroe grumbled as the brother he'd never intended to see again led him into his home.

Jessie gaped at her would-be trespasser as he padded past her, carrying his boots and T-shirt with a bewildered look on his face. If she could just get her jaw off the floor, she might be able to speak.

Linc had a brother? She'd had no idea.

'Can you believe that?' Ali's face beamed. 'I wrote that letter to his old probation officer over a year ago on an off chance. I can't believe he's finally here.'

'His probation officer!' Jessie choked out the words. 'So he really is a criminal!'

'Don't sound so shocked. He was little more than a child when he went to jail. From what Jerry Myers told me, he's been clean as a whistle for the last fourteen years.'

Jessie didn't believe it. Did law-abiding citizens sneak into other people's houses and use their pools? Did they manhandle women they didn't even know? She didn't think so.

'By the way—' Ali sent her a saucy smile '—you guys looked like you were having fun when we arrived.'

Jessie stiffened. 'I thought he was a trespasser or worse. I wasn't having fun. I was trying to get away from him.'

'I see.' Ali looked doubtful. 'So that would explain why he was whispering sweet nothings in your ear, then, would it?'

Jessie's cheeks flamed. 'Actually, he was being rude and obnoxious.' She glared at her sister. 'He was having a ball trying to scare me to death.'

'It serves you right for haring off to confront him in the first place.'

'What?'

Ali waved away Jessie's indignant shout. 'Come on. We better get in there and make sure Linc doesn't let him get away.'

'I'm not going in there,' Jessie snapped back. 'I never want to see That Man again.'

'Jess, you can't avoid Monroe. If Linc and I have our way, he'll be here for a while.'

What was wrong with her sister? Couldn't she see the guy was trouble with a capital T? 'I think you and Linc are insane for inviting him, Ali. You don't even know him.'

The twinkle in Ali's eyes dimmed. 'I'm sorry I teased you. I shouldn't have. What happened by the pool was probably a bit of a shock.'

'I'll say.' At last, Ali was seeing sense.

'But you're going to have to apologise to Monroe about it.'

'You can't be serious.' Was her sister insane? 'I'm not apologising to him. He was trespassing.'

'No, he wasn't,' Ali replied softly. 'We invited him, remember?'

'But that's not the point.'

'Look, Jess. I can't explain this thing with Linc and Monroe to you properly. It's complicated. It has to do with their childhood.'

'Really?' A kernel of curiosity pierced Jessie's anger.

Jessie knew there was something wrong with Linc's family—the only person he'd ever mentioned was his British grandmother who'd died years ago. From the little Jessie knew, he'd spent his summers with her as a child, but he never spoke about the American side of his family and neither did Ali. But still, having met That Man, she wasn't convinced Linc needed to get to know him again. The guy had 'deadbeat' written all over him.

'I can't tell you about it, Jess. Linc wouldn't want me to.' Ali paused, seemed to struggle to find the right words. 'Since we had Emmy, it's been important to Linc to find his brother. He may not be able to have a relationship with Monroe. But the fact that he's here is important. Linc needs to make sure he's okay.'

Jessie looked at her sister and thought she understood.

Ali and Linc were such fantastic parents, they just naturally wanted to watch over everyone. It was the thing she admired most about them. Their devotion to Emmy and to each other had made her yearn for a home and a family of her own.

Jessie didn't think for a minute that the man who had been taking a dip in their pool needed anyone to watch over him. She could see, though, she wasn't going to be able to convince her sister of that. She heaved a sigh of frustration. 'If it's that important, I won't get involved.'

'Jess, you are involved. You're here and so is he. Couldn't you make peace with him? I don't want him to feel uncomfortable. It's taken us years to find him and get him here. I want Linc and him to have a chance.'

Put like that, what choice did Jessie have? Ali and Linc had done so much for her. They'd comforted her when she'd broken up with Toby. She was sure they'd only invited her to stay with them this summer because they'd been worried about her. She could never refuse them anything.

'Oh, all right.' But she'd be keeping her eye on Linc's bad-boy brother. No one took advantage of her family.

'Great.' Ali's eyes warmed. 'Once Linc has helped Monroe

settle into the garage apartment, why don't you go over there with some clean sheets and towels? Show him there are no hard feelings, then you could invite him back to the house for dinner.'

Jessie groaned as her sister waddled off towards the house.

Flipping fantastic! How exactly had she gone from being Bruce Willis in *Die Hard 2* to the welcoming committee from *The Stepford Wives*?

CHAPTER TWO

'NICE place you got here,' Monroe said to Linc as they walked through the lush landscaped gardens towards the garage. Talk about an understatement, Monroe thought. A spread like this must have cost well into the millions.

There had to be at least two acres of grounds. They came to the large three-car garage, nestled at the end of the estate. Monroe was glad to see the two-storey building was a good distance from the main house, constructed in the same wood and glass.

Monroe knew his brother had done well for himself, built his own computer software company up from scratch. Monroe had picked up on a few magazine articles over the years about the Latimer Corporation and its successes. Still, he'd never given any thought to what that meant. His brother was a stranger, so why would he? But now his brother's wealth was staring him right in the face, he could see Linc and he weren't just strangers. They were from different worlds.

'It does the job,' Linc replied mildly.

Linc led the way round the side of the building. Monroe followed his brother up the outside steps.

'Your wife's English, right?' Maybe a bit of polite conversation would help ease the knot in his gut.

'Ali, yeah. We live in London most of the year, her family's there. But we vacation every summer in Long Island. We'll be here through September.'

'Right,' Monroe grunted. No way would he be here that long.

Hearing the affection in his brother's voice as he talked about his family had made the knot in Monroe's gut tighten.

Linc opened the door to the apartment and flicked on the main light switch. Recessed spotlights illuminated the spacious, airy room. With a new kitchen and breakfast bar on one side and a comfortable, expensively furnished living area on the other, the room looked clean, modern and barely used.

'It's only two rooms and a bath,' Linc said.

Two rooms or not, it was the most luxurious accommodation Monroe had seen let alone stayed in for a very long time.

'It's a good thing we had it fixed up over the winter,' Linc said, opening the French doors at the end of the room that led onto a small balcony. 'Or we wouldn't have had a place to offer you.'

Monroe frowned. He needed to put the brakes on, before Linc got the wrong idea. 'It's nice of you to offer. But I don't know if I'll be staying more than a night. I've got stuff to do in New York and I don't have a lot of dough at the moment.'

It wasn't the truth. He'd worked like a dog the last six months so he could afford to spend a few clear months painting. He had stacks of sketches stuffed in his duffel bag that he wanted to get on canvas. He'd had a vague offer to tend bar that came with a room in Brooklyn where he'd been hoping to settle while he got it done.

Painting was Monroe Latimer's secret passion. Ever since he'd taken one of the art classes they'd offered during his second stretch inside, painting had been his lifeline. In those early days, it had been an escape from the ugliness and the sheer boredom of life in a cage. After he'd got out, it was the thing that had kept him centred, kept him sane. He always gave the pictures away or simply burned them when he had to move on. The process was the only thing that mattered to him. Making the oils work for him and putting the visions in his head onto canvas. He didn't need family and possessions. He could put up with the drudgery of dead-end jobs and enjoy his rootless existence, if every six months or so he got the chance to stop and create.

He wasn't about to tell his brother any of that, though. After all, he didn't know the guy.

'Monroe, if you're short right now, surely it'd be good to crash here for a while.'

Monroe stiffened. Pride was the one thing he never compromised. The irony of the situation, though, didn't escape him.

When he'd been sixteen and desperate, after his first stretch in juvie, he'd been prepared to do anything to survive. Mooching off his rich brother back then wouldn't have bothered him; in fact, he would probably have enjoyed screwing the guy over. But in all of the years since, Monroe Latimer had learned a lot about self-control and a whole lot more about self-respect. He'd sworn to himself after that second stretch that he would never go back to that horror again. To do that, he'd stayed clean, and he'd learned to rely on nobody but himself.

'I'm not a freeloader.' Monroe forced the words out, trying to quell his annoyance.

Linc sighed, his voice weary. 'I know that, but you are family.'

'I'm not family.' Monroe watched his brother frown at the words. Tough. He needed to get this straight once and for all. 'We weren't that close as kids, but even if we had been, that was a million years ago. You're not obligated to me any more than I am to you. We're strangers.'

'All right, stop.' Linc held up his hand. 'I understand what you're saying, Roe,' he said slowly. 'Like you say, we're strangers. Don't you think I don't know that?'

'Then why the hell did you invite me?'

'Why did you come?'

The quick rejoinder had Monroe stumbling to a halt. Why the hell had he come? 'I don't know. Just curious, I guess.'

'Well, maybe that's enough for now.' Linc walked across the living area. 'Let me at least show you the rest of the place, before you run out on us.'

Monroe was thinking he should do just that when Linc flung open the door to the apartment's bedroom and his mind went blank.

The wall of glass at the far side of the room flooded it with mid-afternoon light. He could see the pool patio across the gardens, and the ocean beyond. Surf tumbled onto shore on an empty beach of white sand. The view was stunning, but it wasn't that which made his blood slow, his heart thud against his chest. With its walls painted pristine white and only a bed and a small chest for furniture, the room was so bright and airy, he'd never seen a better place to paint. Always before, he'd had to be satisfied with dingy rented rooms or, one memorable summer, a broken-down trailer next to a car dump in Virginia. He'd never had a studio before, had never thought he wanted one, but, seeing the play of sunlight across one wall, he wanted this one.

'You like it?' Linc's question interrupted his thoughts.

'Yeah, I do.' Monroe couldn't disguise the leap of joy in his voice. He refused to let his doubts surface. Couldn't he have this one thing, just for a little while? He'd pay his way; he'd make sure of it. 'Looks like you've got a house guest for a while.'

'Great.' Linc smiled back at him.

'But what I said about being a freeloader still goes.' Monroe walked to the glass and peered down at the garden below. 'You got anyone to do your yard work?'

Linc frowned as he stood beside him, looked down, too. 'No, the old guy who used to do it's having trouble with his arthritis. I figured I'd hire a local kid to keep it under control till Dan gets back on his feet.'

'No need.' Monroe took his eyes away from the window. 'While I'm here, I'll handle it. Looks like the lawn could use a cut. You got a mower in the garage?'

'Yes, but…' Linc's eyes narrowed. 'Monroe, I don't want you doing the yard work. It isn't necessary.'

'It is to me.'

Linc didn't look pleased. 'Fine. I guess I don't have a problem with you cutting the grass every once in a while.'

Monroe figured there were probably a lot of jobs needed doing about the place. From what he'd seen so far, the house and gardens were huge and, oddly for rich folks, they didn't seem to have much hired help. He reckoned if he devoted his mornings to helping out around the place, it'd go some way to paying his brother back for the opportunity to paint in this glorious room.

Jessie replayed her humiliating encounter with Monroe in her head for the thousandth time as she strolled over to the garage apartment, her arms loaded down with fresh linens.

By organising an outing to the local ice cream parlour with Emmy, she'd managed to delay her next encounter with That Man for a good three hours. Unfortunately, out of sight had not meant out of her mind. Of course, Emmy's endless chatter about her 'cool new uncle' over the hot fudge sundaes hadn't helped. But it was the memory of his naked chest pressed against her back that kept slamming back into her thoughts every ten seconds or so. Not to mention all the daft things she'd said and done before that.

Her palms dampened on the white cotton sheets as she mounted the steps to his door. Oh, this was ridiculous. He was just a guy, and a supremely irritating one at that, if their first meeting was anything to go by. She'd promised Ali that she would apologise and that was going to be hard enough, but she absolutely was not going to dissolve in a puddle at his feet as she had almost done by the pool.

Telling the butterflies in her stomach to go away, Jessie tapped on the door. No answer. She raised her fist to knock again when it swung open.

'Oh!' The sight of the tanned naked chest in front of her, glistening with sweat, had her gaping in shock.

'Hey, it's the bad cop. Jessie, right?'

Jessie's eyes shot up to his face. His hair, she noticed, was a dark, burnished blond when it was dry, streaked with gold. With a red and white bandanna tied round his forehead, his tanned, angular face and that thin scar across his brow, he looked like some beautiful Apache sun god, she thought in amazement. Then she spotted the glint of amusement in his riveting blue eyes.

'Don't you ever wear a shirt?' she snapped.

He grinned, sending some really annoying dimples into his cheeks. 'Not when it's hot and I'm doing manual labour.'

'Or when you're pinching a swim in someone else's pool.' The snide remark was out before she could stop it. There was something about the sight of those perfect pectoral muscles, or maybe it was the tantalising sprinkling of chest hair across them, that just seemed to bring out her inner bitch.

'Well…' The cool amusement in his voice made her bristle '…I figure swimming in your clothes is kind of dumb.'

At that precise moment, Jessie recalled exactly what he had—or rather had not—been wearing when she'd first spotted him and her traitorous skin flushed with colour.

* * *

Monroe watched the vivid pink flood her cheeks and grinned some more. No doubt about it, the woman was seriously cute. That mass of curly red hair, which was tied back but hardly tamed, and those round sea-green eyes. With the peaches-and-cream skin and high cheekbones, her face was made up of enchanting contrasts. He glanced down at her slim, shapely legs, showcased by the short skirt of her sundress. Her top half was hidden behind the pile of linens she carried, but he could still remember the feel of her lush breasts pressed against his forearm. She certainly came in one enticing little package.

Jessie hadn't missed the quick but thorough once-over. The flash of warmth and appreciation she'd seen in his eyes wasn't doing a thing for the burning in her cheeks. How humiliating. 'What are you grinning at?'

'Just admiring the scenery.'

Jessie sent him what she hoped was a withering glance. Unperturbed, he leaned forward and plucked the sheets out of her arms.

'Come on in.' He bumped open the door with his butt and strolled into the room.

Jessie stepped gingerly across the threshold. Calm down, woman, and don't show him how much he unnerves you. She was trying to think of a neutral comment when she spotted the bed frame leaning against the far wall. 'What are you doing to the furniture?'

He dumped the sheets on the sofa. 'No need to get ants in your pants. I'm not stealing it.'

Jessie could see the stiff set of his shoulders and suddenly felt ashamed of herself.

She'd promised Ali she'd make peace with him, instead she'd been nasty as soon as he'd opened the door. 'I didn't think you were stealing it,' she said quietly.

'You sure about that?' She heard the humour in his voice, but it didn't quite reach his eyes as he studied her.

She swallowed. 'Of course I am. I was just curious. Is there something wrong with the bed frame?' The intense look in his eyes was making her jumpy again.

He shrugged. 'No, I'm just moving it in here. I've got plans for the other room.'

'Well, that solves that mystery.' She brushed her hands down her dress. 'You're obviously busy. I'll leave you to it.'

'Hey, hold up.' He walked up to her, blocking her exit. 'You're not still pissed about what happened by the pool, are you?'

Of course she was. 'Of course I'm not.'

'You are, aren't you?' That slow, infuriating grin spread across his face, shooting those irresistible dimples back into his cheeks. 'You've got that fired-up look in your eyes.' He flicked a finger at her ponytail. 'Suits you—goes with the hair.'

He was laughing at her again. How infuriating. Jessie put on her best queen-to-serf voice. 'Thank you very much. I don't think I've ever had such an original compliment.'

She tried to walk past him, but he simply reached out and took hold of her upper arm. The warmth of his hard, callused fingers was such a surprise, she yelped.

'Don't panic.' Despite the quiet tone, he continued to hold her in place.

'Let go!' Her voice came out in a breathless rush. He stood so close she could smell him, the musty, but not unpleasant, scent of fresh male sweat.

He dropped his hand, then held the palm up as if in surrender. 'No harm done. I just figured I should say sorry, for earlier.'

The contrite words would be more convincing, Jessie thought, if his eyes weren't dancing with amusement.

She took a quick step back. She really, really wanted to wipe that smile off his face. Tell him he was an overbearing oaf who needed to learn some manners. But she couldn't. His words had reminded her of her promise to Ali.

She was supposed to be apologising to him, not the other way round. Because she couldn't bear to see him laugh at her when she did it, she looked down at her feet. 'That's okay. I guess I was quite rude to you, too.'

She mumbled the words, but when he didn't say anything she was forced to look up. He wasn't smiling any more. In fact, he looked astonished. 'Are you kidding me?'

'No, I'm not.' Jessie bit back her annoyance. Why was he

making this so difficult? 'My sister pointed out that, since you were invited here, you were the wronged party, so I should apologise to you.'

'Is that right?' He tucked his hands into the back pockets of his jeans; his lips twitched. 'So it was big sis that put you up to this. She make you come over with the linens, too?'

Irritated by his perception, Jessie kept her tone even. 'I'm trying to give you a simple and sincere apology. What exactly is your problem?'

'Simple, yeah. Sincere?' He considered the question for a moment. 'I don't think so.'

Jessie glared at him. Sod diplomacy. 'You really are insufferable, aren't you?'

He laughed then, the gesture making his handsome face relax in a way that was ludicrously appealing. Jessie glared at him some more, determined not to notice it.

'Like I said, Red. You're cute when you're mad.'

Jessie's belly tightened at the hot look in his eyes and the gruff way he said the new nickname. 'I'm leaving. I did my best,' she said as she stalked over to the door.

She could hear him laughing harder as she wrenched the door open. She was just about to slam it behind her, though, when she remembered something else.

Turning back, she was dismayed to see he'd followed her. Gripping the door, he leaned against it and grinned down at her. 'What is it, Red? You got something else to apologise for?'

Ignoring the teasing glint in his eyes, Jessie stepped back onto the landing. 'Believe me, that's the only apology you'll ever get out of me.'

'Now that's a shame, when you're so good at it.'

For a deadbeat, he certainly had an answer for everything.

'My sister wanted to invite you to dinner this evening at the house.' She spat the words out. 'About seven o'clock. I'm sure you can find your own way there.'

Duty done, Jessie stomped off down the stairs. Just as she reached the bottom he called after her. 'Hey, Red. You gonna be there?'

She looked back over her shoulder. 'Of course I am.'

He let his gaze drift down to her butt and back. 'Be sure and tell your sister I'll be there, then. I wouldn't want to miss telling her all about that sweet apology you gave me.'

As Jessie stormed off she could hear his deep rumbling laugh all the way past the garage.

CHAPTER THREE

'Did you and Monroe get everything settled, then?' Ali asked as she placed a large plate of cold cuts on the dining table.

'Umm-hmm.' Jessie dropped her head and concentrated on chopping the tomatoes. 'I made my peace with him as requested.' And if he said anything different, she would see to it personally that he suffered.

'And you apologised, for what happened by the pool?'

Jessie suppressed the tug of guilt and dumped the last of the tomatoes into the salad.

'Yes, Ali.' Jessie gave an impatient sigh. 'I apologised to him.' Even though it had nearly killed her.

'And a real nice apology it was, too.'

Both sisters turned to see Monroe standing at the door.

In a newer pair of jeans and a faded blue T-shirt with a Harley Davidson logo, he looked as neat and presentable as Jessie had ever seen him. But as he sauntered into the room with that long, tawny-blond hair, the day-old stubble on his chin and a devil-may-care glint in his eyes, he didn't exactly look safe.

'It's got to be one of the sweetest apologies I've ever had.' He winked at Jessie as he said it and she felt herself flush.

He was laying it on thick to embarrass her. The rat.

'Monroe, I'm so glad you came.' Ali greeted him with a warm smile.

'You're welcome, ma'am.'

'Take a seat and Jess'll get you a drink. I'll just go and get Linc. He's reading Emmy a bedtime story.'

As Ali bustled out of the room Jessie busied herself putting the last of the food on the table. She pretended not to notice as Monroe folded his long frame into the chair opposite.

'A beer would be great, Red.' He said the nickname in a murmur that was deliberately familiar. Jessie looked up. He was watching her, confident and amused. 'Cute dress.' He tilted his head to one side, took a good long look. 'Fits you just right.'

Jessie felt her pulse skid into overdrive. She wasn't sure why she'd decided to change into the figure-hugging silk dress for dinner, but it certainly hadn't been to see that flare of heat in his eyes.

'I'll get your beer.' She walked stiffly to the fridge. The low, masculine chuckle from behind her made her jaws tighten. Where were Linc and Ali? If she had to spend much longer alone with him, she'd dump the beer on his head.

Jessie didn't miss the teasing heat in Monroe's gaze when she plunked the glass of beer in front of him. Lounging in the chair, his lean, muscular physique looked magnificent. Her pulse thudded against her neck. Why did all the best-looking men have the most aggravating personalities?

'Thanks, Red.' He picked up the glass; one brow lifted as he eyed the huge foam head. 'Looks like you need a little practice with your bartending skills, though.'

She smiled sweetly at him. 'I'm sorry to say I don't have the time. I'm too busy making obsequious apologies to people who don't deserve them.'

He barked out a laugh just as Linc and Ali walked into the room.

'Monroe, good to see you.' Linc held out a hand. 'I hope Jessie's making you feel at home.'

'She certainly is,' Monroe said smoothly as he stood up and shook his brother's hand.

As they all settled down to eat, Jessie couldn't resist sticking her tongue out at him from behind her sister's back. He winked back, making her regret the childish gesture. She'd ignore him, she thought, as she picked up her knife and fork. Now, if only she could swallow, too.

Monroe thought the dinner would be stiff and formal, but he found it surprisingly easy to talk to his brother and sister-in-law.

He hadn't eaten since a stale bagel that morning in an interstate truck stop, so the mouth-watering selection of salads and cold cuts also went down well.

He'd expected lots of probing questions about what the hell he'd been doing all this time while his brother had made a staggering success of his life. Instead Linc and Ali kept their inquiries discreet and when he didn't elaborate they seemed more than happy to take up the slack, telling him funny stories about their family and how they'd first met.

Monroe hadn't missed the intimate looks that passed from husband to wife during the telling. He also noticed the way his brother never seemed to miss an opportunity to touch his wife.

The gentle, possessive hand resting on the small of her back when she sat down to eat. The way his fingers stroked her arm when she passed him the salad bowl. The love between them was so tangible, Monroe was touched despite his determination to remain aloof.

Monroe liked watching people. It helped him create the pictures he painted. But while he could see the love between Linc and his wife, he was more interested in the reaction of Ali's sister. He had seen the shadow of longing in Jessie's eyes.

When Linc and Ali left the table to get the dessert, Monroe kept his eyes on Jessie. She watched the couple walk over to the large open kitchen together, the yearning in her eyes obvious when Linc pulled his wife into a fleeting embrace behind the breakfast bar. What was Jessie thinking, he wondered, with that romantic look in her eyes?

She turned suddenly, and caught him studying her.

'Will you stop staring at me? It happens to be flipping rude.'

It was the first time she'd spoken to him directly since handing him his beer. The exasperation in her voice made him smile.

'So's swearing at the table, Red, but you don't hear me complaining.'

Would she never be able to get the last word with this man? Jessie thought as her teeth ground together.

To her surprise, the dinner hadn't been as excruciating as she thought it would be. For an ex-con and obvious reprobate he could be charming when he wanted to be. Although she noticed he'd been cleverly evasive whenever Ali or Linc had asked him about his life. He just said he'd been 'on the move.' Well, okay, she didn't exactly have a spectacular career at the moment, but she did have goals, objectives. At the very least, she did a bit more than just travel around on a motorbike.

She'd also caught him staring at her several times during the meal. That last probing look, when she'd been daydreaming about having a marriage like Linc and Ali's, had really unsettled her. The strange sense of envy she felt was one of her most shameful secrets.

'Flipping is hardly a swear word,' she whispered, so Linc and Ali wouldn't overhear them. 'It's just an expression.'

'Red, anything's a swear word when you say it with that look in your eye.'

She choked down her pithy response when Ali appeared with a huge lemon pie.

'I hope you've still got some room left, Monroe,' Ai said, placing the pie on the table.

Monroe leaned back and patted his flat belly. 'I might just have a little.'

The pie was served as soon as Linc arrived with a gallon of ice cream. Avoiding Monroe's gaze, which seemed to be fixed on her yet again, Jessie gave Linc her sweetest smile. 'I thought I'd go into town tomorrow and beg the people at the Cranford Art Gallery for the Saturday job they've been advertising. Could I borrow the BMW?'

'Sorry, Jess.' Linc scooped some more ice cream onto his plate. 'It's making a weird noise. I'm planning to get the guy at the shop to take a look at it.'

'I'll give it a look.'

Linc stopped eating at Monroe's casual comment. 'There's no need.'

Monroe forked up another generous piece of pie, sent his brother a level look. 'Sure there is.'

Jessie could see Linc was on the verge of refusing again, when Ali touched his arm, silencing him. Ali beamed a smile at Monroe. 'That's great, Monroe. It'll save us the trouble of having to call the mechanic.'

Jessie wondered at the sudden tension in the room between the two men. It was also odd that Monroe had made the offer. After all, wasn't he supposed to be a deadbeat? She shrugged the thought aside; it made no difference to her what he was. She turned to Ali. 'Are you using the people carrier tomorrow?'

Ali nodded. 'Linc and I promised Emmy we'd go to the funfair at Pleasance Beach. Maybe we could drop you off in town and then pick you up later. Did you have a particular time in mind?'

'It's okay. That'll take you miles out of your way.' Jessie couldn't help feeling a little crestfallen. She'd wanted to get to the gallery tomorrow. She needed to find a job.

'You can catch a ride with me on the Harley,' Monroe said. 'I've got to go into town and pick up some groceries. I've got a spare helmet.'

Jessie stared at him. Surely he couldn't be serious. 'No, really, it's no problem. I'll go in another day.'

'Don't be silly, Jessie,' Ali piped up. 'If Monroe's offering you should—'

'I couldn't possibly trouble him like that,' Jessie interrupted her sister and aimed a telling look at Monroe. His lips curved slowly. Why did she suddenly feel like a mouse being stalked by a tomcat?

'No trouble. No trouble at all.' He stood up, smiled at Ali. 'Thanks again for the dinner. It was delicious.'

'You're welcome.' Ali beamed at him as Linc rose and offered to see him out.

Just as he got to the door, Monroe turned and gave Jessie another of those winks that made her pulse scramble.

'See you in the morning, Red. Better put on some pants, though.' His gaze crept down and then back up, making her face heat. 'That little bit of a dress won't wear too well on the Harley.'

Jessie scowled as his tall frame strolled out the door ahead of Linc. How annoying that he'd gone and got the last word in again.

CHAPTER FOUR

THE next day dawned bright and clear, the sluggish heat kept at bay by a cool breeze off the Atlantic.

Jessie got up with Emmy, made a quick breakfast of cereal and toast for them both, and then handed her over to Linc and Ali. From the flushed look on her sister's face after the lie-in Jessie had promised the couple, it looked as if they hadn't been doing much sleeping.

Jessie ignored the stab of envy as she went upstairs to have her shower. Her sister had a fabulous marriage to a fabulous man. When Jessie had been a bridesmaid at their wedding, she'd known that theirs was the ideal marriage—full of passion but grounded in a deep, abiding love. It was the sort of marriage Jessie wanted for herself.

So far, though, things hadn't quite worked out that way.

It had taken her two long years and one broken engagement to realise Toby was about as far from her ideal mate as it was possible to get. She had thought he loved her, when the only person he really loved was himself.

She'd tried so hard to persuade herself that Toby was 'the one.' When he'd asked her to marry him, she'd been swept up in the romance of the moment. But the minute she'd said yes, a little voice in her head had started telling her to run like mad in the opposite direction. She'd been naïve and immature; she could see that now. The huge sense of relief when they had finally gone their separate ways had made Jessie determined never to make that mistake again. However glad she'd been to see the back of Toby, the relationship had left her with the depressing thought that she might never find what Ali had.

Heck, at twenty-six she'd never had halfway decent sex, let alone great sex. When Toby had accused her of being frigid, she'd had to accept that he might well be right. He'd never once stirred the passion in her that Linc so obviously stirred in Ali. She hadn't so much as kissed a guy since she'd hurled Toby's engagement ring at him six long months ago. Worse than that, she hadn't even wanted to.

Determined not to let the creeping sense of despair take hold, Jessie wrapped the towel around her and walked to the closet. After careful consideration, she picked out a chic but simple shift dress with large sunflowers on it. She needed to look hip and stylish if she was going to persuade the art gallery to take her on as a Saturday assistant. Cranford might be a small seaside town, but it was no backwater. A tourist Mecca for the Hamptons' super-rich and aspirational summer residents, the gallery and its clientele would be as sophisticated as any you'd find in Uptown Manhattan.

Jessie had promised Ali that she'd help out with Emmy until the family went back to London in September. But she hoped to get a Saturday job to earn some much-needed money in the meantime. Linc had insisted on paying all her expenses to get her over here, but Jessie didn't want him giving her spending money as well. He'd already tried to give her a credit card, which she'd flatly refused, but in the end she'd persuaded him to help her get a temporary working visa. Also, a job in an art gallery was just up her street. She loved art, and, while she'd accepted she didn't have the talent to be an artist herself, she had always hoped to whittle out a career in the art world. She'd spent six long months drifting since the breakup with Toby. It was time to get her life back on track. Ali handled her life calmly and competently, Jessie thought. If she wanted what Ali had, she needed to start doing the same.

At that thought, the memory of Monroe Latimer watching her in the dining room the night before, his pure blue eyes alight with amusement, blasted into her brain and wouldn't get out again. Jessie frowned. He might have the goods in the looks department, but luckily for her she was not a shallow person. It hadn't taken her long to see he was a long way short of her ideal mate in every other department. Flirtatious, arrogant and dangerously attractive, he could make any woman lose sight of what was really important. And for Jessie that was the long haul, not the quick flash-fire of sexual attraction.

Remembering Monroe's parting comment about the proper bike attire with not a little irritation, Jessie slipped into the dress and then pulled on a pair of jeans. She'd just have to take them off when she got to town. After dabbing on some lipstick, Jessie slipped a pair of yellow slingback sandals into her bag and tugged on her sneakers. She tied her hair into a ruthless ponytail and checked herself in the room's full-length cheval mirror.

Yep, she looked preposterous.

At least her daft get-up should stop Monroe staring at her in that disconcerting way. She wasn't looking forward to riding on his bike. Despite all his shortcomings, she had the uncomfortable feeling that being pressed up against that muscular back for the ten-mile ride into town might stir feelings she didn't want stirred. Quite why she was more sexually aware of him than she had ever been of any other man didn't bear thinking about.

'Damn it!' Monroe pulled his hand out from under the car's hood and watched the blood seep out of the shallow scrape.

'Did you hurt yourself?'

Turning at the voice, Monroe watched Jessie walk across the garage towards him. She should have looked ridiculous with denim on under the floating, flowery dress, but she didn't. She looked chic and summery. His eyes dipped to her cleavage, demurely displayed above the dress's scoop neck. Sucking the blood from his knuckle, he took in every detail.

'I certainly hope it's not fatal?' The sharp note in her voice suggested she hoped exactly the opposite. He grinned as his gaze lifted back up to her face.

Pulling a bandanna out of his back pocket, he leaned against the car's hood. 'You know, Red,' he said as he wrapped the cloth round his hand, 'that figure of yours would look great in just about anything.' And even better out of anything, Monroe thought, enjoying the way her eyes narrowed in irritation.

Trying to ignore the way her pulse was racing, Jessie fingered her bag strap and glared at him. 'While your fashion advice is certainly invaluable, I can see you're busy. Maybe I should come back later.' Or not at all, she added silently, already feeling unpleasantly flustered.

'No need.' He pushed up from the car's hood. 'I'll go clean up and then we can head out.' He walked towards her, forcing her to tilt her head back. 'It'd be a shame not to, Red. Now that you're all dolled up.'

She watched him mount the steps to his apartment. He made it sound as if she'd dressed up especially for him. The conceited jerk.

Monroe took less than ten minutes, but Jessie was just about to walk off, her heart rate still hitching uncomfortably, when he reappeared. He had a fresh white T-shirt on, the same worn jeans, a small plaster on his hand and a motorbike helmet slung over his arm.

'This is for you.' He handed her the helmet. 'The bike's out front.' As she turned to walk ahead of him she felt his palm on the small of her back. The minimal contact made her jump.

'Easy, Red.' He lifted his hand. 'Just being polite.'

Jessie didn't think so, from the mischievous twinkle in his eyes, but didn't trust herself to speak. When they reached the bike, she fumbled for a moment trying to put her helmet on, before he lifted it out of her hands.

He did a circular motion with his finger. 'Turn around.'

She did as he asked, grabbing her hair when he deftly removed the band holding it in a ponytail. 'What are you doing?' she demanded as his fingers combed through her hair.

He put his hands on her shoulders and turned her to face him. 'It'll be more comfortable like that, with the helmet on.'

He rewarded her scowl with another heart-thumping smile as he placed the helmet on her head and fastened the strap. The light brush of his fingers seemed to burn the soft skin under her chin. This was going to be a nightmare. She hadn't even got on the bike yet and already she felt as if she were about to explode.

Unhooking his own helmet from the handlebar, he put it on and then climbed onto the enormous machine. 'Hop on, Red.'

It took several attempts before she managed to clamber up

behind him. She had to push her feet hard on the footrests and grasp the back of the seat to stop from sliding against him. She was grateful for the jeans now, because her dress had ridden right up to her waist.

'I'm ready,' she said, feeling like an idiot.

Instead of starting the machine, he took his hands off the handlebars, pulled off his helmet and turned round. 'You ever ride a motorcycle before, Red?'

'Well, no, not exactly.' She didn't like that smug look in his eyes.

'First rule, hold on tight.'

'I am holding on tight.' Her knuckles ached, she was gripping the seat so hard.

He shook his head. 'Not onto the bike, sweetheart—onto me.'

'Why can't I just hold onto the bike?' She could hear the whine in her voice, but couldn't help it. She didn't want to hold onto him.

'Because when we hit a curve, you're going to have to lean with me.' His lips quirked. What was so amusing? 'Wouldn't want you falling off.'

He was talking to her as if she were an imbecile. 'Fine. I'll hold onto you.'

He grinned, the dimples winking in his cheeks, before he turned and put his helmet back on. To her utter shock, he reached behind, put two large hands on her thighs and dragged her towards him. Before she could blink, she was snuggled against him, her legs spread wide to accommodate his denim-clad butt.

'Now, put your arms round my waist.'

She didn't want to, but what choice did she have? She wrapped her arms round him, tried to ignore the feel of his hard, flat stomach beneath her palms. His back felt firm and warm against the thin silk of her dress. He pushed back to kick the bike into life. The powerful vibrations of the machine rumbled up through her thighs, making Jessie painfully aware of all the places where their bodies touched. The very core of her started to throb. How humiliating. His shoulder shifted as he gripped the clutch and her nipples hardened. Worried that he might be able to feel them, she wriggled back, but his hand simply came round again and pulled her back.

'Stay put, Red, and hold on.'

As soon as he shouted the words at her, the big black machine started to roar up the small hill. Although it was probably only going ten miles per hour up the drive, Jessie tightened her grip on him, grateful for the solid, sure feel of him in front of her. As the breeze caught the ends of her hair beneath the helmet she pressed into his back.

By the time they hit the main coastal road, Jessie couldn't have cared less if she were naked behind him. The exhilarating feeling of speed and freedom as the scenery whizzed by around them and the wind whipping at her arms and face was fantastic. She loved roller-coaster rides but this was better. Every time they leaned into a bend, her stomach leapt up into her throat and she gripped onto his waist even tighter. He felt wonderful, warm and strong and unyielding. She could smell the clean scent of his cotton T-shirt and the subtle hint of soap and motor oil. The hard, sculpted muscles of his butt rubbed against her centre every time he moved his foot on the gears and her nipples were so hard now she was sure they were boring a hole in his back.

Despite the intimacy, the devastating effect he was having on her physically, she sighed when they drove into the main thoroughfare of town, disappointed that the ride was over so quickly. He slowed the bike down to a gentle purr as he drove through the wide, tree-lined main street of the picturesque seaside town, finally pulling to a stop in front of the grocery store.

Jessie took a moment before peeling herself off him and leaning back. He tugged off his helmet, and a huge grin split his face as he turned round. 'What did you think?'

'It's fantastic!' Her voice was muffled by the helmet but giddy with pleasure.

'You liked it, huh?'

She nodded, grinning back at him. As she tried to undo the helmet strap with shaking fingers, he brushed her hands aside and did the job for her, lifting it off her head. 'You're a real biker chick now, Red.'

The feel of her lush body wrapped around him had made Monroe's jeans uncomfortably tight, but he couldn't help smiling at the look of pure pleasure on her face. Seeing a small mark on her forehead, he rubbed it softly with his thumb. 'Looks like you could do with a better helmet, though.'

'Don't worry about that. It felt wonderful. Everything felt wonderful. It was so exciting. No wonder you've spent all those years riding around on your motorbike.'

There was no censure in her words, none of the disdain that she had shown him last night, only joy and enthusiasm. With her emerald eyes sparkling, her hair curling wildly and the pink glow of pleasure flushing her cheeks, she looked gorgeous.

He wanted to kiss her so badly it hurt.

Stunned by the sudden reckless urge, Monroe swung back round and concentrated on attaching the helmet to the handlebars.

'You better climb down first,' he muttered.

Jessie stared at his back as she hopped off the Harley. What had happened? One minute he'd been smiling at her, enjoying the moment with her, and then, all of a sudden, he'd as good as dismissed her.

She adjusted her bag as he lifted his leg over the bike.

'Thanks for the ride. It was…' She babbled to a halt, seeing the intensity in his eyes as he turned to her. She wetted her lips with the tip of her tongue and his gaze shot down to her mouth. 'It was really fun.' The words came out on a feeble whisper. What was going on here? Why was he staring at her mouth like that? She felt light-headed and she didn't know why.

'You're welcome, Red.' The nickname sounded anything but casual. 'See that diner?' He nodded across the street. 'I'll hang out there when I'm finished till you're ready to head back.'

The instant thrill at the thought of being back on the bike with him was followed by uncertainty. Maybe she'd enjoyed the ride too much.

'I might be a while.'

'Take all the time you need. I'm in no hurry.'

As Jessie walked away from him she was sure she could feel his eyes following her all the way down the street.

After an hour of trying to sell herself to Mrs Belinda Bennett, the proprietor of the Cranford Art Gallery, Jessie was frazzled. She'd chewed off most of her lipstick during the interview, but the hard sell had been worth it. Mrs Bennett had agreed to give her the job of Saturday sales assistant on a trial basis.

Feeling worn out but enthusiastic, Jessie forgot to feel nervous as she wandered into the small coffee house Monroe had indicated. She spotted him immediately, lounging in a booth opposite the door. He looked relaxed and gorgeous with a few sacks of shopping on the seat opposite.

'Hi.' She waved. 'I hope you haven't been here long.'

He slid out of the booth as she walked up to it. 'Not long. I was about to order pancakes.' His gaze took a leisurely journey down to her feet, now encased in the flattering yellow sling-backs, and then came back up again. Jessie's nerves came back full force when he smiled. 'It looks even better without the denim,' he said.

'Thanks.' Her voice quivered annoyingly as she slipped into the booth.

'Move over,' he said.

She'd expected him to lift up the bags opposite and sit there, but instead he pushed onto the bench seat beside her, nudging her with his hips. When he leant back and put his long, muscled forearm on the seat behind her, she realised she was totally boxed in.

'So how did it go—you get the job?'

'Yes, I start on Saturday.'

'Hey, way to go.' He patted her shoulder. 'How about we order pancakes and coffee to celebrate?'

'That would be lovely, thanks.'

He seemed genuinely pleased for her, so she tried not to notice the way his long, firm thigh was touching her leg. The thin silk of her dress did nothing to protect her against the warm pressure.

As he ordered two short stacks with coffee for them, Jessie noticed the way the teenage waitress blushed profusely. Did he have that potent effect on every woman he met?

'Looks like you've been busy, too.' She nodded at his purchases, spotting the logo of the town's expensive art supply shop. 'What did you get at Melville's?'

'Sketching charcoal, a couple of brushes, stuff like that.'

'Do you paint, then?'

'Sure, a little.'

'Really? That's wonderful. Are you any good?'

He took his arm away from behind her, looked away. 'I don't know and I don't really give a damn.'

The statement was abrupt and rude, and so out of keeping with his usual easygoing manner, Jessie felt instantly contrite. Somehow she'd insulted him.

'I'm sorry.' She touched his arm. 'I only asked because I love art and I'm absolutely useless at it myself.'

He glanced down at her fingers, gave a stiff jerk of his shoulders. 'No harm done.'

'Here you go, folks, two short stacks straight up.' The teenager beamed at Monroe as she placed the pancakes and mugs of coffee in front of them.

'This looks great, Shelby.' He smiled at the girl, reading the name off the blue tag on her uniform. Jessie watched the waitress flush again before she rushed off.

'What sort of things do you paint?' Jessie asked quietly as Monroe concentrated on drowning his plate in syrup.

He didn't reply. She waited as he swallowed a generous helping of pancakes and syrup. He nodded towards her plate. 'You not hungry?'

'I was just wondering about what you paint,' she repeated, feeling a little foolish now but determined to get an answer out of him.

'I haven't done any yet.'

'Yes, but, when you have, what will you paint?'

'They don't taste as good cold, you know,' he said, looking at her plate again.

Jessie remained silent. He wasn't meeting her eyes. Why was he being so evasive? But as she watched him take a sip from his coffee it occurred to her. He was shy about his artwork. It seemed so unlikely, but it was the only answer that made sense. The thought made him seem vulnerable, all of a sudden, maybe even a little bit sweet.

She waited. Finally, he stopped eating, turned to her. 'Look, it's no big deal, all right? It's just a dumb hobby.'

'I'm still curious what sort of painting you do. I mean, is it abstract, expressionism, more traditional like portraiture, landscapes? I'm really interested in art. Looking at it, appreciating it, visiting art galleries—those are a few of my dumb hobbies.'

He let out a breath, put down his fork. He *was* shy. He looked almost as uncomfortable now as when Ali had identified him at the pool the day before.

'It's mostly people, landscapes, any stuff that catches my eye and I want to put it on canvas. But you won't see any of it in an art gallery, that's for sure.' He eyed her plate again. 'If you don't want them, I'll eat them.'

'Okay, okay, I'll eat them.' Jessie picked up the maple syrup and swirled it over her stack, feeling ridiculously pleased that she'd managed to get him to talk about his artwork. After finishing a mouthful, she smiled at him, her mouth sticky. 'Mmm, these are delicious.'

Licking her lips, she caught the quick flick of his eyes down to her mouth. Her belly tightened. Okay, so maybe sweet wasn't quite the right word for him.

Having insisted on paying for their pancakes and leaving what Jessie thought was an excessive tip for the smitten Shelby, Monroe guided her out of the coffee shop.

Given that he lived on a shoestring and had very few possessions, she thought it odd that he was so generous with his money. She began to feel a little ashamed about what she'd said to Ali yesterday. He might be poor, but he was no deadbeat.

She had watched his hands while they ate. Long, thin fingers and wide palms—they were really beautiful. He had an artist's hands. She wondered again about what sort of things he painted. He'd neatly steered the conversation away from his artwork after she'd started eating and she'd let him, even though the subject intrigued her enormously. Not just because she loved art, but because his unwillingness to speak about it had made him seem a lot less cocksure and confident.

She could feel the pressure on the small of her back from his palm as he steered her out of the diner. She couldn't ignore the warmth in her middle at the contact. He still made her nervous. Men as good-looking as he was would always make her feel a little inadequate. Then there was that aura of wildness and danger about him that was unlike anyone she had ever known before. But she had to admit that he was starting to fascinate her.

They walked across the street in silence, but as they reached the bike Jessie remembered her bare legs. 'Would you mind waiting a minute while I go and put my jeans back on?'

He glanced at her legs. 'Sure. Seems like a shame, though.'

She was busy quelling the little flutter of excitement at his words when she spotted a familiar face coming out of the grocery store. 'Oh, no.'

Monroe gave her a quizzical look as he opened the saddlebags on the back of the Harley. 'What's the problem?'

'It's Bradley Dexter. I don't want him to spot me,' Jessie whispered as she ducked behind Monroe.

Bradley Dexter III was the son of Linc and Ali's nearest neighbour. Pampered and idle, he thought his red sports car was an extension of his personality and had turned out to be as persistent as a woodworm after Jessie had met him on the beach a few weeks before. She might be hard up, but she was not *that* hard up.

Jessie realised she was too late to avoid another annoying encounter, though, when the well-muscled young man in the surfer's standard uniform of board shorts and vest-top walked up to them. 'Hiya, Jessie. How'ya doing?'

Monroe heard the sigh from behind him before Jessie appeared at his side.

'Hello, Bradley.'

'We've got a beach party going tonight at the Sunspot. You wanna come along?' The guy's eyes dipped down Jessie's frame in a way Monroe didn't like one bit. 'You could wear that bitching little bikini I saw you in last week.'

Monroe thought he could hear Jessie's teeth grinding together. 'That's nice of you, Bradley, but I think I'm busy.' She touched Monroe's arm. 'This is Monroe, by the way. Monroe Latimer—he's Linc's brother.'

Bradley gave Monroe an absent glance. 'Sure, nice to meet you, dude. I guess you could come, too. But I get first dibs on the babe here.' He winked at Jessie, the hunger in his eyes unmistakable. Seeing Jessie blush and stiffen, Monroe felt his anger rise.

He put a firm hand on Jessie's hip and pulled her to his side. Ignoring her quick intake of breath, he gave Bradley a sharp stare.

'I don't think so, dude.' He had the surfer's attention now. 'I don't share.'

Bradley stepped back, his Adam's apple bobbing. 'Sure, man, no problem.' He gave Jessie a nervous wave, his gaze fixed on Monroe. 'See ya 'round, Jess,' he said and scurried off.

'What was that about?' Jessie shrugged off Monroe's arm.

'I was getting rid of Bradley the wolf for you.'

'I don't need your protection, thank you.'

Miserably embarrassed, Jessie stepped past Monroe but was pulled up short when he put his hands on her hips, tugged her into his arms. 'He's looking back,' he whispered in her ear as he nuzzled her neck. Shock waves shot through her whole system. 'Let's show him we mean business.'

'What?'

Jessie had no chance to react. No chance to register his intent. Strong fingers combed through her hair, angled her head slightly and then his lips were on hers. The move was so smooth, so fluid, Jessie could only gasp before his mouth covered hers.

The contact was electric. His mouth was firm and commanding on hers, his tongue exploring and then retreating in a clever rhythm that robbed her of thought. He kept one hand on her head, anchoring her to him, while the other swept down, moulding her curves before settling firmly on her bottom and pulling her even closer.

The rough feel of his jeans against her legs, the strong, solid feel of his chest against her breasts were so unyielding she felt as if she were being smothered. Her response though was unstoppable. Her mouth opened wider as her tongue tangled with his. He lifted his head for a moment and her breath gushed out, but then his lips were back on hers again. His teeth bit into her bottom lip. She began to pant, feeling dazed, delirious.

Then, suddenly, it was over.

'There.' His voice sounded dim because of the blood pounding in her ears. 'That ought to convince him.'

Jessie blinked up at him, her face flooding with heat as she registered the words through the fog of arousal. It was as if she'd been doused with ice water. She shoved him, her arms still shaking from need. 'You bastard.'

He held onto her arm. 'What's wrong, Red?'

She was so angry she could have spat at him. He was smiling at her, as if it had all been a game. The terrible tug of need and desire still throbbing in her belly only made her feel more humiliated. 'You had no right...' Her voice shook. 'You had no right to do that.'

Monroe could see the sheen of moisture in her eyes and hated himself for it. He wanted to taste her again. God, he wanted to strip her naked and bury himself inside her. Her response to the simple kiss had been electrifying. He was hard as a rock and throbbing painfully in his jeans. It was a major struggle to keep the carefree smile on his face. 'I was just trying to help you out with Bradley. What's the big deal?'

It was a lie. He'd wanted to kiss her ever since he'd laid eyes on her. That he'd been unable to resist her wasn't something he wanted to admit, though, even to himself.

'I didn't ask for your help.' Jessie's words came out on a broken sob. Desperate not to let him see her break, she struggled out of his grasp.

'No harm done. It was just a little kiss.'

He made it sound like nothing at all. It would only make her seem like an idiot if she let him see how much more it had meant to her. Biting her lip to keep the tears back, Jessie gripped the strap of her bag with unsteady fingers. She had to get away from him.

He tucked a finger under her chin, his eyes clouded with concern. 'Hey, I'm sorry.'

Was that pity in his eyes? Jessie pushed his hand away, forced her eyes to go flat and remote. 'It's okay, Monroe.' She'd made enough of a spectacle of herself already. 'Like you said, it was nothing.' She whirled away from him.

As Jessie walked towards the public restrooms she kept her head high, her back ramrod straight, but couldn't stop the silent tears of humiliation rolling down her cheeks.

* * *

The journey back to the house was agony for both of them.

As Jessie clung onto the back of the bike, refusing to hold onto Monroe, she felt none of the thrill from the earlier journey into town.

All she could think about was the kiss they'd shared. It had been like no other kiss she'd ever had before. She'd made love before with less excitement.

Why had she responded to him like that?

It was mortifying and, what was worse, it had meant less than nothing to him. 'What's the big deal?' —that was what he'd said. He must have kissed loads of women before her and she hadn't measured up very well. He hadn't even insisted that she hold onto him on the ride back as he'd done on the way there. She felt angry with him and humiliated, but worse, much worse, was the feeling of rejection that she couldn't seem to shake no matter how hard she tried. Why should she care what a womanising ex-con thought of her? But the problem was she did care.

Monroe wanted to kick himself for his stupidity. Why the hell had he kissed her? Now he knew what she tasted like, what she felt like in his arms, he was going to have a hell of a time keeping his hands off her.

He had to keep his hands off her.

He slept with women for mutual pleasure, for kicks, but it could never mean anything deeper than that. He never got involved with anyone who might mean more to him. That was the way he lived; that was the way he had to live. Free and easy. No commitments, no ties.

The way she'd looked at him after the kiss, the shattered horror in her eyes had touched a place inside him he'd never even admitted existed. The woman was bad news all round. He was going to have to keep well clear of her. But how the hell was he going to do that, when he wanted her so damn much?

CHAPTER FIVE

'JESS?'

'Over here, Al.' Jessie poked her head round the kitchen counter as her sister waddled into view.

'Do you think you could get Emmy for me? I'm so tired.'

Seeing the exhaustion on her sister's face, Jessie dashed over and took her arm. 'Sit down, for goodness' sake.' She guided Ali towards the sofa. 'Where is Emmy? I thought she was with Linc.'

'He's working today, some crisis at the New York office.' Ali settled into the cushions and gave a hefty sigh. 'Emmy's been camped over at Monroe's all morning.'

Jessie frowned. 'But I thought she went over to see him yesterday.'

'And the day before that.' Ali paused to rub her back. 'She's been helping him fix the BMW. You wouldn't believe the state of her clothes when she got back yesterday. I was worried Monroe might be getting tired of having her hanging around. But I think he was actually pleased to see her this morning.' She smiled, her eyes warm. 'Anyway, I thought maybe you could go rescue him, as lunch is nearly ready.'

'Um.' Jessie felt trapped.

She'd been avoiding Monroe for over a week. If the humiliating memory of their kiss wasn't bad enough, the fact that she'd been reliving it in her dreams every night had made it all seem so much worse. She still wasn't ready to see him again. But Ali looked shattered. She couldn't very well refuse such a simple request.

Jessie arranged the sandwiches she'd made on the table, tried to steady her breathing. 'I'll go get her in a minute, Al.'

'Why don't you ask Monroe if he wants to come over for the barbecue tonight?' Ali said from the sofa. 'I haven't been able to tempt him with any of my invitations so far, but maybe the promise of a medium-rare steak will do the trick.'

Jessie's cheeks coloured. She'd rather gnaw off her own foot than ask Monroe over for the family's evening barbecue. All she needed was his smouldering looks over the charcoal to put her right off her own steak.

She rustled up a sweet smile for Ali as she slipped on her sandals. 'Will do.'

It was an effort for Jessie not to curse out loud as she marched across the lawn to the garage apartment. She was just pondering how she could get away with not giving him Ali's dinner invitation when she heard the delighted peal of Emmy's laughter, followed by a gruff masculine chuckle.

Rounding the side of the garage, she spotted Monroe's long jeans-clad legs sticking out from under the car. All she could see of Emmy were two pink sneakers wiggling furiously.

Should she be shocked or amazed that he actually had her five-year-old niece doubling as a car mechanic?

There was a loud clanging sound.

'Hey, hold on there, kid.'

'Sorry. Did I break it?' Emmy's feet went still.

Monroe's reply wasn't annoyed, just amused. 'Nah. It's tougher than that, but just remember what I said.'

'Treat the car with respect and it'll respect you back.' Emmy said the words as if reciting holy scripture.

'You got it. You want to finish it?'

'Can I?'

Jessie frowned at the adoring tone of her niece's voice. Did every single female within a ten-mile radius have to fall at his feet?

'Go for it.' She heard Emmy's childish grunt before Monroe's deep voice continued. 'That's it, kid. You're a great mechanic. Why don't you haul out? I'll be right behind you.'

Jessie stepped back as Emmy crawled out from under the car.

'Oh, Aunt Jessie, Aunt Jessie.' Emmy leapt in the air. Her face, which was smudged with what could only be axle grease, glowed with excitement. 'I did a lube job. It was way cool. Uncle Roe showed me, he let me do it all by myself.'

'That's wonderful, Emmy.' Jessie tried to sound enthusiastic but couldn't help wincing at the huge oil stain all over her niece's favourite Barbie T-shirt. 'We better go get you washed up before lunch.'

'Do I have to go?' Emmy's chin hit her chest. 'Uncle Roe said I could have peanut butter and jelly sandwiches with him today.'

Jessie was just wondering how to deal with that request when the man himself slid out from under the car and got to his feet. Her heart thudded in her chest at the sight of him, tall and lean in ragged denim and faded cotton. She could feel her face getting hot at the long look he gave her and wanted to scream.

'Hi, Red.' There was that stupid nickname again. The heat in her face increased.

'Hello, Monroe.'

Jessie was grateful when Emmy tugged on his jeans, distracting him.

'Jessie says I've got to go now, but I want to have lunch with you.'

He kneeled down, gave the little girl a serious look as she rested her hands on his shoulders. 'Don't sweat it. We can do that another time.'

Jessie saw Emmy had left grubby fingerprints all over him, but Monroe didn't seem to notice as he held onto the little girl and stood up. The shadow of emotion crossed his face. For a moment he seemed lost in thought, but then his eyes focused on Jessie and he gave her a slow smile that made her feel unpleasantly warm.

'We'll go clean up,' he said. 'You want to come up and grab a drink?'

The statement sounded casual, but they both knew it was an olive branch.

Jessie wanted to stay mad at him; the memory of the kiss they'd shared still loomed large between them. But having seen the tender, thoughtful way he handled Emmy and the beaming grin on her niece's face as she clung to his neck, she just couldn't do it.

'That would be nice, thanks.'

As he turned to heft the little girl up the stairs to his apartment, Jessie wondered at this new, nurturing side of him she never would have expected. She followed them up the steps, trying to stop her eyes from straying to the very nice male butt displayed in front of her in worn denim.

Entering the apartment, Monroe let Emmy scramble down out of his arms. 'You know where the soap is, kid.'

'Yes, Uncle Roe.' She shot him an impish grin and scampered off to the bathroom.

Monroe felt an answering squeeze on his heart. He didn't have any experience with kids, but Linc's daughter had really gotten to him in the last few days.

He wasn't supposed to be making any attachments. He was just passing through. But when the little girl had hugged him round the neck a few minutes ago and settled so easily into his arms, the trust and adoration in her eyes had made his heart hurt in a way that couldn't be good

Of course, the sight of Emmy's auntie, looking gorgeous and irritated, hadn't exactly made the emotional punch any easier to deal with.

Jessie had been avoiding him for the last week or so, ever since that incendiary kiss of theirs in town, and he'd been more than happy to let her.

The woman was a major complication—one he definitely didn't need. Over the last few days, his mind had strayed to thoughts of her without warning. The minute he'd seen her again, he'd had to admit he'd missed her. The woman looked good enough to eat and, now he knew what she tasted like, it was hard to resist taking another bite.

He heard her step into the apartment and close the door, but concentrated on washing his hands and pouring himself a long, cold glass of water.

If Emmy's sweet, uncomplicated affection was getting to him, it was nothing compared to the effect the kid's auntie was having on him. And one thing was for sure, his thoughts in that direction were a lot more dangerous. He turned, appreciating the way her hips moved as she walked into the room.

'Emmy's certainly taken a shine to you,' she murmured.

'I've taken a shine to her, too. She's a great kid.' He raised his glass. 'Do you want a glass of water? It's all I've got.'

'That would be nice.'

'No problem.' He pulled another glass from the cabinet above the sink and filled it. 'Here you go.'

She took the glass, her hand trembling as their fingers touched.

Her eyes met his and he watched as the heat crept into her cheeks. Yep, it was going to be near on impossible to keep his hands off her now.

Jessie took a hasty gulp of water and spluttered as the cold liquid hit the back of her throat.

'You okay there, Red?' His voice was low and intimate.

He put his hand on her back and rubbed. She was positive she could feel the calluses on his fingers through the thin cotton of her dress and she shivered. Get a grip, woman.

'I'm finished, Uncle Roe.'

The little girl skipped back into the room, unaware of the tension that sizzled between the two adults.

'All clean?' Monroe said the words to Emmy but kept his eyes on Jessie.

'Yes, look.' Emmy held up her hands for Monroe's inspection. Jessie released the breath she'd been holding as he turned to look at the little girl.

'Good job.'

Emmy ran up and grabbed hold of his leg. 'Can I come back tomorrow? Can I? Can I?'

He ruffled the little girl's curly brown hair. 'Sure, if you want to and your mom says it's okay.'

'We better be going, Emmy.' Jessie reached for her niece's hand, but the little girl continued to cling onto her uncle. 'Lunch is already on the table.'

'Okay.' Emmy let go reluctantly and put her hand in Jessie's.

'I'll see you tomorrow, kid.' Hearing the affection in Monroe's voice, seeing the warm way he rested his hand on Emmy's shoulder, Jessie felt a sharp surge of guilt.

She had no right to keep this man from bonding with his family.

So what if she couldn't stop blushing every time she saw him? So what if she couldn't seem to forget that kiss? From what she could gather, Linc and Ali and Emmy were the only family Monroe Latimer had. Not giving him Ali's dinner invitation suddenly seemed both cowardly and selfish.

'Ali wondered if you'd like to come over for dinner tonight,' Jessie blurted out. She saw surprise flash in his eyes, but he said nothing. 'We're having a barbecue. Linc's doing steaks…' Her voice trailed off when Monroe remained silent.

'Come, come, come.' Emmy jumped up and down as she sang the words. Jessie was grateful that her niece had picked up the ball, but could see Monroe was still hesitating.

'I don't know.' He sounded oddly unsure of himself.

'We'd all love to have you there,' Jessie said, surprised to realise she meant it.

His gaze intensified. 'You would, huh?'

'We would, we would, we would,' Emmy sang again. He gave her a quick grin before he looked back at Jessie.

'I guess it'd be my pleasure, then. I can't say no to two pretty ladies.'

Emmy giggled and then shouted, 'Yippee,' punching the air with her small fist.

Jessie felt the same leap of joy, despite the ball of heat that seemed to have lodged beneath her breastbone.

'I'll tell Ali.' Jessie gave Monroe a shaky smile as she pulled Emmy towards the door.

'Bye-bye.' Emmy waved.

'See you tonight, kid. You, too, Red.'

Jessie glanced back. He was leaning against the kitchen counter. He looked relaxed again and amused, his thumbs hooked into his jeans and a ridiculously charming smile on his face. Jessie felt the fire blaze inside her. Unable to trust her voice, she gave him a quick nod as she hauled Emmy out the door.

No question about it, Monroe thought wryly as he watched Jessie close the apartment door. The woman was dangerous.

He strolled across the apartment to the French doors and watched as Jessie and Emmy made their way up to the house.

Emmy was skipping ahead, while Jessie walked behind, looking lush and unbearably sexy in the tight little polka-dot number.

Dangerous or not, she was becoming damn near irresistible. She looked gorgeous, and he loved the way she blushed so easily. But it wasn't just her appearance or her obvious reaction to him that made her so appealing.

He also liked her as a person. She was full of spirit and fire and feisty as hell.

Maybe they could have a little fun together after all. She was a grown woman who certainly knew her own mind and didn't mind speaking it. She was obviously unattached and in need of a little romance or she wouldn't have kissed him the way she had in front of the grocery store. He'd already made it clear that he was just passing through, so there was no need for her to get the wrong idea.

He leaned against the glass as Emmy and Jessie disappeared from view. Maybe he'd test the waters tonight, see how she responded to the suggestion. His lips curved as he thought about what he and Jessie could do to amuse each other over the next month or so.

CHAPTER SIX

'GET a grip, woman!' Jessie stalked over to her wardrobe.

The cerise linen dress she shoved back in was the fourth outfit she'd tried on in less than twenty minutes. Staring into the snarl of colours and fabrics, she resisted the urge to stamp her foot.

What on earth was the matter with her?

Why did she care what Monroe thought of her outfit anyway? Determined not to waste any more time on a decision that should have taken her ten seconds, she grabbed the first thing that came to hand.

You could never go wrong with the old little black dress, she thought as she slipped the slinky Lycra sheath over her head.

She examined herself in the wardrobe's full-length mirror, caught her bottom lip between her teeth. Was the outfit maybe a little too sexy for an evening barbecue with her family? She could picture Monroe's lazy smile. The hot look in his eyes.

Stop it, you silly cow. The LBD was fine; he probably wouldn't even notice that the material clung a little too closely to every curve.

She never should have invited him. She'd known this was going to happen. She slammed the wardrobe door and slipped on a pair of simple red pumps. She pulled a matching silk scarf from the array in her dresser and tied it loosely round her neck. She might have guessed she would blow this completely out of proportion.

She didn't know what it was about Monroe, but whenever she was near him she was so brutally aware of him she couldn't seem to think about anything else but the feel of his lips on hers. His long, strong body pressed against her. It was ridiculous—they'd only shared one kiss and he'd made it quite clear that, for him at least, it had just been play-acting. But her flustered response when their fingers had touched over the water glass that afternoon went to show she could not be trusted to keep her cool around him.

She was a grown woman. She did not have crushes. She'd just never been kissed like that before and she still needed a bit more time to settle.

The way she was feeling at the moment, twenty-five years probably wouldn't be long enough.

Jessie stepped out into the hallway and closed the door to her room. Relax and breathe, she told herself as she walked stiffly down the stairs.

Jessie was both relieved and disappointed when she walked out onto the terrace and saw that Monroe wasn't there yet.

The night was balmy and warm and the smell of jasmine hung in the air like a rich woman's perfume. The fairy lights Linc had rigged up over the barbecue winked in the dusk and reflected off the surface of the pool like cheeky little water nymphs.

The fluttering in her stomach calmed as she strolled round the water to the grill. As Linc lorded it over the flames with a pair of barbecue tongs, the mouth-watering scent of cooking meat surrounded him.

Looking up, he caught sight of her and smiled. 'Hey, good-looking.'

The tightness in Jessie's chest eased, the familiarity of family making her feel safe and secure. 'That should be my line, shouldn't it?' She gave Linc a light kiss on the cheek. 'As in what you got cookin'?'

'About a half a cow,' Linc joked. 'I hope you're hungry.'

Where once the teasing admiration in her brother-in-law's eyes would have had Jessie blushing profusely, now she simply felt a warm, comfortable feeling settle in.

'Stop flirting with my sister and watch what you're doing,' Ali called out from behind them. 'I don't want burnt cow again, thank you very much.'

Jessie turned to see her sister flopped in a large armchair.

Emmy giggled, glancing up from the jigsaw she was piecing together by her mother's feet.

'Stop your belly-aching, woman,' Linc replied, giving Jessie a conspiratorial wink.

Jessie grinned back at him, then sat down in the chair next to her sister. 'Still feeling exhausted?'

Ali adjusted herself in her seat and huffed. 'No, not really, I just have this devilish urge to make Linc's life hell at the moment.' The twinkle in her eyes was positively wicked. 'After all, he's the one responsible for this.' Ali laid her palms heavily on the impressive mound of her belly.

'The way I heard it,' Jessie leant in and whispered to her sister, 'he wasn't the only one there.'

Ali laughed and gave her a light slap on the arm. 'Hey, you're supposed to be on my side. And by the way, while we're talking about sisterly solidarity,' she continued, giving Jessie's figure a quick appraisal, 'it would help if you didn't look like a supermodel while I look like a beached whale.'

'Thanks, I think,' Jessie replied.

'Mummy, when's Uncle Monroe going to be here?' Emmy's sleepy enquiry made Jessie's pulse spike.

'Soon, honey,' Ali replied, her voice relaxed. 'What time did you tell him, Jess?'

'I don't remember. But he can see the pool terrace from his bedroom window, he must know we're out here.'

'Good point,' Ali remarked, eyeing her sister thoughtfully. 'You know, it's funny,' Ali continued, her voice suspiciously light, 'but I've noticed it's only your invitations that he accepts.'

Jessie's head swung round, the gaze that had strayed up to Monroe's apartment window focused on her sister again. 'What are you trying to say?'

'Nothing. Just that he's quite a hunk, isn't he?'

'I…I guess so,' Jessie sputtered, seeing the sharp look on her sister's face. She tensed. This was what she'd been afraid of. Did her sister think she was developing some sort of ridiculous crush on Monroe?

Ali touched Jessie's arm, her voice softened. 'I happen to know from experience, Jess, that the Latimer men are hard to resist.'

'I don't know what you mean.'

'All I'm saying is, if you need to talk, I'm here.' Ali smiled, patting her rounded belly. 'In fact, I'm anchored to the spot.'

Linc had started piling the steaks onto a large serving plate when Jessie spotted Monroe's tall figure strolling towards them in the darkening twilight.

Emmy scrambled out of her lap. 'Uncle Roe!' The little girl dashed across the lawn towards him, her drowsiness forgotten in a spurt of excitement.

Jessie watched as Monroe swung his niece up in his arms.

'Emmy's certainly fallen for him,' Ali murmured next to her. Jessie didn't dare turn round, worried her face had the same adoring look on it that Emmy's did.

Monroe hefted Emmy easily into his arms, enjoying her sleepy commentary on the 'hours and hours and hours' she'd been waiting for him. She clung to his neck, her light breath on his cheek making him feel good and at the same time strangely uneasy.

He'd watched the little group on the pool terrace from his apartment window for nearly half an hour before coming over. He'd almost decided not to come at all.

He hadn't been able to hear what they were saying, but they looked from where he'd been standing like a unit, a family. His brother's family, he'd thought, and the sharp sense of envy had stunned him. He didn't want this sort of life, this sort of commitment, so why did their comfortable companionship tug at some place deep inside him?

He'd accepted Jessie's invitation earlier because he enjoyed watching her. He'd told himself it was a nice healthy dose of lust that had dragged him out tonight.

But now, with Emmy's little fingers clinging onto his neck, the comforting warmth in Ali's eyes as she greeted him, the friendly handshake Linc gave him as he walked up to the grill, he realised that it wasn't only lust. The feeling of warmth, of need, scared him.

'Just in time.' Linc's voice was easy, confident. Why did Monroe feel so out of his element?

'Jess,' Linc said, 'grab Monroe a beer from the cooler—looks like he's got his hands full.'

Monroe's eyes settled on Jessie as she handed him an icy bottle. He shifted Emmy in his arms to take it. 'Thanks, Red.'

She gave him a quick nod then looked away, but he'd seen the flash of awareness and what looked like worry in her face. He couldn't take his eyes off her as she took the steaks from Linc and placed them on the long glass table laid out on the patio.

Her hair seemed to be made of flame tonight, tumbling down her back in wild, lustrous waves. The simple little black number she had on should have been demure but it showcased the curves beneath in a way that was damn near indecent. Aware that Linc might be watching him, Monroe took a long pull of his beer and dragged his eyes away.

'We might as well get settled,' Linc said quietly.

Emmy laid her head on Monroe's shoulder. The little girl went still and heavy in his arms as Linc and Ali and Jessie put the last of the food on the table. The feel of Emmy's body relaxing against his made the ache in his heart sharpen.

Linc placed a hand on his daughter's back. 'Come on, Emmy. You can sit in my lap while we eat.'

'I want to stay with Monroe,' Emmy's tired voice whispered against Monroe's neck.

'It's okay, Linc. She's no trouble,' he found himself saying.

'You sure? It's not that easy slicing steak with a sleeping child in your arms.'

Monroe simply nodded. He didn't know why he wanted to keep the child with him. He just knew he did.

Jessie watched as Monroe struggled to finish his food. Emmy was sound asleep in his lap. Linc and Ali had started clearing the table. The meal had gone quickly, Linc and Ali keeping the conversation light and undemanding. Monroe had been surprisingly subdued.

Something had changed about him. The cocksure, devil-may-care confidence that seemed so much a part of him was gone tonight. The same vulnerability she'd glimpsed in the diner was back tonight. Why did he seem wary and unsure of himself?

'I feel stuffed.' Ali sighed and leaned back in her chair.

Linc gave her belly a reassuring rub. 'That's because you are, honey.'

Ali swatted his hand. 'Not funny, Latimer.'

Linc laughed and hauled her out of her chair. 'Come on, I'll take the plates in and you can put your feet up on the sofa.' Putting an arm round his wife, Linc smiled at Jessie and Monroe. 'You want me to take Emmy, Monroe?'

'She's out like a light. I can hold her a while longer.'

'Thanks.'

Jessie stacked all the plates except Monroe's and handed them to Linc.

As Linc and Ali walked off across the lawn, Jessie settled back into her seat and watched Monroe. The pungent aroma of the dying charcoal was overlaid with the rich scent of summer blooms and the crisp smell of the sea. She could hear the gentle hum of the surf on the beach, and the soft murmur of Emmy's childish snores.

It occurred to Jessie that for some reason during the evening her nerves had simply dissolved. The night had settled around them, comforting yet also intimate, but she didn't feel nervous about being left alone with Monroe. Maybe it was the two glasses of wine she'd had, she thought, as she took another sip. Or more likely it was the sight of him with the little girl curled in his arms. Tonight, for the first time, he didn't scare her.

When his knife clattered onto the plate again, Jessie took pity on him. 'Do you want me to cut it for you?'

He looked up, his brow creasing. 'Yeah, thanks, I'm starving.'

Leaning over, Jessie began slicing the meat on his plate.

'I feel like a first-grader.' His voice whispered close to her ear, making the soft skin of her nape tingle. But unlike before, when the giddy awareness had made her feel vulnerable and irritated, she enjoyed the warmth that seemed to spread up her neck.

'I could take her in.' She pushed his plate back to him. 'She probably ought to go to bed now anyway.'

'No need.' He adjusted the little girl in his lap, forking up a mouthful of the newly-cut meat as Emmy's head nestled against his broad shoulder. He chewed and swallowed. 'It's kind of nice to hold her when she's not talking a mile a minute.' He looked a little shocked at his own admission, making Jessie's lips curve.

'What's so funny?' The prickle of annoyance in his tone made Jessie's smile widen.

'You are. You're cute.'

He frowned at that, putting down his fork. 'Hey, that's my line.'

'Not any more, it's not.' Jessie nodded at Emmy. 'She's totally besotted with you, you know.'

'She's a good kid.' He sounded confused, making Jessie wonder.

'She's also a very good judge of character.'

Monroe blinked at the statement. The soft words sounded almost like an endearment. He studied Jessie in the flickering light. He'd planned to come on to her tonight. An opportunity like this, with her as good as flirting with him, should have been just what he was looking for.

He wanted to kiss her in the worst way. But something was holding him back. And it wasn't only the sleeping child in his lap.

He didn't only want to feast on those sweet lips of hers, he realised with a jolt. He wanted to bask in the approval he saw in her eyes. He wanted her to care for him. That was the problem. He felt the stab of guilt at the thought. He'd intended to seduce her, not make her fall for him. That would never work.

'She doesn't know me.' The words came out harsher than he'd intended. 'And neither do you, Red.'

The abrupt statement might have put Jessie off, but as he said it she could see the panic in his eyes. He wasn't angry. Not really. He was scared. But why?

'Does it frighten you, Monroe, to have people care about you?'

She knew she'd struck a nerve when he stiffened. Annoyance swirled in his eyes. 'What the hell does that—' The angry words cut off when Emmy stirred.

He rocked her gently, until the child settled again. When he looked back at Jessie, she could see he'd been careful to settle himself as well.

The slow, easy smile that she knew so well spread across his face. But for the first time she realised it was nothing more than a diversionary tactic. A defence. The lazy grin his way of distancing himself.

'Don't get the wrong idea, Red.' His tone was low and intimate, making the familiar shiver run up her spine. 'I won't mind a bit if you want to get up close and personal with me. In fact, I'm counting on it.'

He was teasing her again, but it didn't make her bristle as it once had, because she could see the usual twinkle hadn't reached his eyes. Enjoying her newfound power, Jessie raised a coquettish eyebrow and looked him straight in the eye.

'That's quite a challenge, Monroe. I'd be careful if I were you. I might take you up on it.'

She could see she'd surprised him when his eyes widened, but the surge of heat that followed made her breath catch. He was looking at her now as if he wanted to devour her. Suddenly the giddy fluttering in her belly, the heat in her cheeks from an hour before were back with a vengeance.

He might be cute, but she'd be a fool to think he wasn't still dangerous.

'Jess, you want to grab the rest of the plates while I put Emmy to bed?' Linc's voice came to Jessie through the blood pounding in her ears. She forced her eyes away from Monroe to see her brother-in-law walking round the pool towards them both. She let out an audible breath.

Saved, she thought, and in the nick of time.

Jessie sat at the vanity table in her room and slathered moisturiser on her face. As had become a habit over the last week, her gaze strayed out her bedroom window, across the dark expanse of the gardens to Monroe's garage apartment. As always, his windows were a beacon of light in the night. She glanced at the clock on the mantelpiece. Nearly midnight again. Did the man never sleep?

She closed the curtains, shrugged into the simple satin shift she wore to sleep in and turned the switch by the door. The air conditioner subsided to a quiet hum. She walked across the room and sank into the huge double bed. As she pulled the thin sheet over herself she couldn't stop thinking about the apartment across the way and the man inside it.

He still made her nervous. After all, no matter what she did, she just couldn't forget that kiss. But despite that, tonight, and maybe even before that, her opinion of him had changed. She knew now there was a lot more to him than his staggering good looks and his industrial-strength sex appeal.

Over the past week and a half Jessie had let go of her suspicion that he had arrived on Linc's doorstep to sponge off his rich brother.

Monroe had spent every morning since he'd been there either tuning up the cars or working on the garden. He'd fixed the lawn-mower and, after ten days of his tender loving care, the grass was at last green again and the flowerbeds were starting to perk up, too. And all this, even though Linc had told him again at supper that he was a guest and should act like one. Monroe had simply shrugged and said that he liked helping out.

He disappeared every afternoon, and apart from tonight had refused all of Ali's invitations to come to supper. Jessie wondered what he was doing right now. Maybe he was in bed, too. The thought sent a shaft of heat straight to her core.

Get a hold of yourself. She was acting like a woman with a serious problem. But Ali was right, he was a hunk, and right at the moment he seemed to be focused on her. She began to think about the other things she knew about him, and then shot upright in bed.

He wasn't in bed, now. He was painting. Of course, that was what he had to be doing.

If she hadn't been distracted by that kiss and her newfound feelings for him she would have remembered their conversation in the diner sooner.

Throwing off the covers, Jessie paced to the room's *en suite* bathroom and ran herself a glass of water. What did he paint? Whether or not he had any talent, he was certainly dedicated. He was at it every afternoon and most of the night.

Draining the glass, Jessie rinsed it out and walked back across the deep pile carpet to the bedroom window. She peeked out of the curtains. She felt silly, like an over-eager schoolgirl, fantasising about her first major crush and spying on him in the middle of the night. But she couldn't help it. This intriguing new turn of events only made him all the more irresistible.

His lights were still on.

She was dying to see what he was doing. After all, art was her passion, too.

When she'd left college, she'd kidded herself for a whole year that she was destined to take the art world by storm.

After a series of rejections, though, from a string of different galleries, she'd had to admit that, although she was passionate about art, her talent—like her portfolio—had been woefully inadequate.

It wasn't that she was dreadful; she just wasn't ever going to be great. Being able to see her own inadequacies had been her curse, she'd thought this spring, when she'd finally given up her job as a layout designer in a tiny print shop in Soho.

She'd been miserable doing the mundane, boring designs for pamphlets. Not only did it waste what little design talent she had, it was also a million miles from the beauty and elegance that she'd once hoped to embrace.

When Ali and Linc had asked her to come out to America for the summer and help out with Emmy while Ali awaited the birth of her second child, she'd jumped at the chance. It would be a chance to forget about her miserable failure with Toby as well as her pathetic attempt to start a career as a designer. Linc had also arranged a working visa, so she could 'keep her options open,' as he put it.

Being with Ali's family had lifted her spirits and now that she had her new job at the little gallery in Cranford, she finally felt as if she weren't spinning her wheels any more. She was starting afresh at last. Time to get a new master plan. Maybe this was where her talent lay—in the appreciation of art.

Jessie let the curtain fall back down. But how the heck was she going to make a life's work out of it if she had an artist living in the same house as her—or as good as—and it had taken her over a week to figure it out? Okay, so she had been slightly distracted by other things where Monroe was concerned, but really. It was totally pathetic.

Whipping the sheet back and climbing into bed, Jessie was struck by the sight of Monroe that evening when he had said goodbye to her. That cocky grin back in place.

Well, okay, so Monroe had a pretty devastating effect on her, but she ought to be able to ask the guy to let her have a look at his work. Fluffing up her pillow, she plopped her head down on it. She would march over to his apartment tomorrow when she got back from work and demand to see what he was painting. How hard could it be?

CHAPTER SEVEN

'MONROE, we need to talk.' Linc's face was set, his voice firm.

'Yeah, what about?' Monroe raised an eyebrow. He didn't like it. They were standing in the kitchen of the main house. It was Saturday morning and, after the unsettling feelings stirred at last night's barbecue, the last thing he needed now was a brother-to-brother chat.

'Here.' Reaching into the fridge, Linc took out two frosty Pepsis and handed one across the breakfast bar. 'Take this and sit down.'

Monroe hooked a leg over the stool and opened his soda. He took a long drag, he'd been repairing the deer fencing most of the morning and his mouth felt as if he'd been chewing sand.

'What's the problem?' Monroe was glad to hear the easy confidence back in his voice.

Jessie had spooked him pretty bad the night before with that crack about him being scared of people caring. He'd spent the night painting—and thinking hard about what she'd said. It had taken a while for him to sort it out—too damn long, in fact—but everything was cool now.

Why should Jessie's comment bother him? She didn't know him. Nobody did. By the early hours of the morning, he'd managed to dismiss what she'd said and think about what had happened after.

Jessie had made it pretty clear she might be interested in a little fun. Given that, and the fact that she turned him inside out with lust, it was going to be impossible for him to ignore her for much longer. But fun was all it would be. Simple and uncomplicated. He could give her a good time. He just had to make sure she understood fun was all it would be.

'I want you to stop mowing the lawn.' The sharp tone of Linc's voice brought Monroe back to the matter at hand. Linc took a sip of his Pepsi, the movement jerky and tense. 'And tuning the damn cars, and working so hard around the place, for heaven's sake.'

'The BMW needed a tune.' Monroe kept his tone casual. 'I can't believe you'd treat such a beautiful machine with such little respect.'

Linc slammed his can down, knocking over one of the framed snapshots perched at the end of the breakfast bar. 'The damn car's never run better in years. That's not the point and you know it. You're a guest here. I don't want you working to pay your way.'

Monroe took another sip, watched his brother over the rim. 'I'm not a freeloader, Linc. I told you that from the get-go. Either you accept the work or I'm out of here.'

'Hell.' Linc drank down the last of the small can, crushed it in one hand and flung it in the trash.

Hearing the resignation in his brother's voice, Monroe relaxed as he put his own soda down. As far as he was concerned, the matter was settled. He reached for the photo that had fallen over. Flipping it upright, he studied the picture inside.

It was a wedding shot, but not the stiff formal type. Ali looked sexy and happy in a full-length white dress while Linc stood behind her. He was wearing a black tux, but the tie was gone, the top few buttons of his dress shirt were undone and his arms were wrapped around his bride's midriff. The smile on his face was relaxed and proud. The rest of the wedding party was arranged around them, all grinning or laughing at the camera.

'Nice shot,' Monroe said as he stared at the snapshot, ashamed at the familiar tug of envy.

Linc leaned across to take a look. 'Ali's dad took it. It was a great day.'

Monroe could hear the bone-deep contentment in his brother's voice and struggled not to feel jealous. He absolutely refused to go there again.

It was then he spotted the vivacious figure in a clingy fire-engine-red dress at the far left of the picture. The bold colour should have clashed with the mass of dark red hair, but instead it displayed the young woman's soft, translucent skin and luscious curves to perfection. Before he could stop himself, Monroe ran his thumb gently down the image.

'Jess is a real stunner, isn't she?' Linc murmured.

'What?' Monroe looked up to find his brother watching him. 'I guess so.' He put the photo back where it belonged. He could see the frown on Linc's face and knew why it was there. 'No need to worry, bro. I know she's out of my league.'

Linc frowned. 'What makes you think that?' he asked quietly.

Monroe lifted an eyebrow. 'Oh, come on.' He shrugged, tried to sound indifferent. 'Even I can see that girl's got commitment tattooed across her forehead in block letters and you and I both know I can barely spell the word.'

Linc's eyes narrowed. 'Why can't you spell it, Monroe?'

Monroe drained the last of his soda and glared at his brother. 'I don't know, Linc.' He couldn't keep the bitter edge of sarcasm out of his voice. 'Maybe because I was in juvie when I should have been graduating high school.'

Monroe stood up, his face rigid. Angry that his brother had made him lose the comfortable distance he'd struggled so long for the night before. Angrier still that he'd been forced to lie to Linc. Jessie might be out of his league, but he was going after her anyway.

Linc looked at him coolly for a moment before speaking. 'What's so scary about commitment, Monroe?'

Monroe's jaw tensed, his brother's words too damn reminiscent of what Jessie had said to him the night before. Didn't any of these people get it? His thoughts and feelings were his business and nobody else's.

'I'm not scared of commitment,' he snarled, and then stopped. Calm down. Keep it cool. Don't let him see he's rattled you. 'I'm just not interested in it.'

'Jess is, so you should be careful there, Roe,' Linc said evenly. 'You could hurt her.'

'I'm not going to hurt her.' To hell with keeping it cool. 'And anyway, it's none of your damn business.'

Sending the empty soda can sailing into the trash, Monroe stalked out of the kitchen.

* * *

Linc watched as his brother stormed off across the lawn towards the garage apartment, temper evident in each long, angry stride. He shook his head slowly, and smiled. 'That's where you're wrong,' he said gently. 'We're family, Roe. And that makes it my business whether you like it or not.'

'Hey, Monroe.'

Monroe caught Ali's shouted greeting over the roar of the lawnmower and switched off the powerful machine.

He struggled for patience as she walked towards him. He didn't want company. It had taken him most of the morning to calm down after his run-in with Linc.

As he watched her approach his eyes skidded down her figure. It had been dark last night and he hadn't got a good look at her. But now in the noon sun, her belly looked enormous in the stretchy little summer dress. Embarrassed that he found the sight beautiful, he looked away. He concentrated on pulling the bandanna out of his back pocket and wiping his brow.

Drawing level with the riding mower, Ali sighed and rubbed her back. 'You're just the man I needed to talk to.'

Monroe dismounted slowly. 'You got me.'

His glance seemed to flit to her abdomen again of its own accord.

Ali smiled. 'Don't panic, Monroe. I'm not due for at least another few weeks.'

Monroe felt his stomach pitch. 'You're gonna get bigger?'

She laughed. 'Probably, but don't worry. I won't pop.'

Monroe spent some time tucking his bandanna into his back pocket before looking at her. He could see the smile in her eyes and relaxed enough to smile back at her.

She didn't just look big. She looked gorgeous. Her sister Jessie would look the same when she had kids. He ruthlessly suppressed the thought. It wasn't something he was ever going to see.

'Anyway, enough about me and the bump,' Ali remarked. 'I wanted to thank you for all the work you've been doing around here. The people carrier drives like a dream now and the gardens look fantastic.'

'You're welcome.' His shoulders tensed. 'Linc hasn't sent you over to tell me to stop, has he?'

'No.' She looked surprised. 'Did he have words with you about it, then?'

'Yeah.' It annoyed him to realise it was still needling him.

'I thought he might,' Ali said slowly, a considering look in her eyes. 'Linc's a little hung up about money. He thinks because he's got heaps of it, nobody else should pay for anything. He's generous to a fault,' Ali continued, the calm understanding in her face making Monroe feel edgy. 'But he doesn't always stop to consider the importance of pride and self-respect. Especially to people who've had to earn it the hard way.'

Monroe was speechless. How the hell did she know that about him? They'd only met a week or so ago.

'Anyway—' Ali's voice was light, but the look in her eyes as she registered his reaction was anything but '—I didn't come to talk to you about Linc and his many shortcomings.'

Monroe tried to shake off his uneasiness. 'Right.'

'Linc's got a problem at the New York office, so we've decided to base ourselves at the penthouse for a few weeks. We're leaving tomorrow evening.'

'No sweat.' Did that include Jessie? he wondered.

'The thing is, it's Emmy's sixth birthday next Tuesday.'

Monroe gave a quick grin, recalling Emmy's endless chatter on the subject. 'She might just have mentioned that a couple of times.'

'I'll bet she has.' Ali grinned back. 'We thought it might be nice, before we head off to Manhattan, if we had a little surprise birthday party for her tomorrow afternoon.'

'Sounds like a plan.' Monroe refused to feel the little stab of pain as it occurred to him why Ali was telling him all this. 'You want me to make myself scarce. It's not a problem.'

'What? No!' Ali grabbed his arm. Her eyes, Monroe saw with amazement, were wide with shock. 'Monroe, for goodness' sake! I came staggering all the way out here—and, believe me, walking three hundred yards with a belly this size is no mean feat—to make sure you didn't make yourself scarce tomorrow. I want you there. Emmy would be devastated if you didn't turn up. We all would be.'

Now it was his turn to be amazed. He could see by the earnest look in her eyes that she was absolutely serious. 'Are you sure about this?'

'Monroe, I'm warning you, if you don't show up, I'm going to—' She broke off, grabbed her belly. 'Oh!'

Monroe felt the blood drain out of his face. 'What's wrong, Ali? Is it the kid?' He reached for her, but Ali only grinned when she got her breath back.

'No, no. It's okay.' She kept hold of his hand, pulled it towards her. 'The baby gave me the most almighty kick. Here, press down and you can feel it, too.'

She placed her hands over his and pushed his palm firmly into the stretchy cotton fabric. Monroe was about to draw back, miserably embarrassed, when he felt two quick jabs.

'Damn!' His heart jumped into his throat.

'Isn't it great? This one's a real slugger. Emmy used to just lie there all day. I guess she made up for it, though, when she got out.'

Lost in happy memories, Ali didn't look at him until he dragged his palm away.

Her face sobered instantly. 'Monroe, are you okay?'

'Yeah.' He felt sick with regret and a terrible longing that he thought he'd buried years before. 'It's just…it's pretty mind-blowing, isn't it?' That much was at least the truth. 'I need to get back to this. I'll see you later.'

Ali watched as Monroe climbed back onto the ride-on mower. Why was he avoiding her eyes? And why had he looked so shattered, so desperate, a moment ago? 'Don't forget, I want to see you at the house tomorrow, around about noon,' she said.

'Sure.' He gave her a vague nod as he pulled the bandanna out of his back pocket and tied it round his forehead.

'And I better warn you, I won't accept any excuses.' Her parting words were lost in the roar of the engine. Ali could see the grim concentration on his face as he drove off.

What had happened to him? And what did it have to do with the baby?

CHAPTER EIGHT

As JESSIE wrote out her third delivery slip of the day, she saw the Cranford Art Gallery's owner, Mrs Bennett, approach.

'Well done, my dear,' she said. 'I can't remember the last time we sold three canvases in the space of a couple of hours.' It was the first time Jessie had seen Mrs Bennett really smile. The gesture made her look younger and even a little carefree.

Jessie found herself smiling back. 'Thank you, Mrs Bennett.'

'You know, you're a natural at this.'

'I think I've been lucky with the sales,' Jessie said, cautiously.

'I'm not talking about the sales,' Mrs Bennett said. 'Although, that is a nice side benefit. No, I mean, you know about art. You've got a good eye, my dear.'

Jessie found her chest swelling at the appreciation in her employer's gaze. She'd been distracted since last night, thinking about Monroe and his artwork. Wondering if she even had the right to ask to see it. Would she really know if it was any good or not? But Mrs Bennett's praise gave her a newfound confidence. Maybe her idea that she could make a career out of her appreciation of art wasn't that ridiculous after all. 'Thank you, that means a lot to me,' she said.

'I'm glad.' Mrs Bennett leant forward. 'Actually, my coming over to speak to you wasn't entirely altruistic.'

'It wasn't?'

'Ellen Arthur just rang to say she's sprained her ankle.'

'That's dreadful.' Jessie knew the other woman was the gallery's chief sales assistant and part-time curator.

'It's not all that serious, but Ellen won't be in for the next two weeks and I need someone to cover for her in the mornings. I wondered if you could come in?'

'I'd love to,' Jessie answered instinctively, then remembered her conversation with Ali that morning. 'Oh, but I can't—I'm supposed to be going to New York with my sister and her family tomorrow.' After all, she'd come to America this summer to help out Ali and Linc. 'But I suppose I could speak to my sister about it.'

'Why don't you call her, dear, and find out if she needs you there?' Mrs Bennett sounded undaunted. 'I'll pay you Ellen's hourly rate and it will be a good opportunity for you to look at the rest of our stock. I need some advice about what to hang now you've managed to sell ten paintings in the space of two weekends.'

It wasn't until after she had confirmed with Ali it would be okay for her to stay in the Hamptons that it occurred to Jessie what else Mrs Bennett's impromptu job offer would mean. She'd be spending a fortnight alone with Monroe. Okay, so he'd be in his garage apartment and she'd be in the house, but she had as good as issued an ultimatum to him yesterday evening at dinner. What would she do if he decided to take her up on it? That the thought was exciting as well as terrifying could not be a good sign.

Jessie was debating that fact when Mrs Bennett strolled into the gallery's tiny office.

'Is it all settled, then?' she said.

'Yes, I'm okay to stay.'

'Excellent. Now, you're needed out on the floor—a very attractive young man's just strolled in. Either he's penniless or he's the first beatnik I've seen in twenty years, but, either way, it's never wise to ignore a customer.'

Jessie was walking out into the exhibition space, contemplating what the next two weeks alone with Monroe could mean, when her mouth dropped open.

Monroe Latimer was standing staring at one of the gallery's largest seascapes. His hands were tucked into the back pockets of ragged jeans, his head tilted to one side as he studied the work. He didn't just look attractive. He looked mouth-watering—and ridiculously out of place in Mrs Bennett's ritzy little art gallery. That combination of cute and dangerous could well be her undoing, Jessie decided as every nerve ending in her body stood to attention.

Taking a deep steadying breath she walked over to him. Challenge or no challenge, they were going to be the next best thing to room-mates for two whole weeks and she had to learn to deal with him. She also had the little matter of his artwork to work on, too. The perfect opening had just presented itself and she wasn't going to be a coward and ignore it.

'So, what do you think of it?'

As Monroe turned and saw Jessie standing behind him, his first thought was he'd made a big mistake. In the businesslike silk suit, her wild hair pinned up, she looked ridiculously prim and pretty. The urge to tug the pins out, feel the gilded flaming mass fall through his fingers, was almost uncontrollable.

He'd been offkilter, out of sorts the whole day, thanks to Linc and then Ali and even the unborn baby. It seemed the whole damn family was working against him, forcing him into a place he didn't want to be. It made him feel trapped, but much, much worse, it made him feel wanted. He didn't like it.

He didn't know what impulse had sent him into town to see Jessie.

Somehow, the thought of seeing her had buoyed his spirits. Even when she'd messed with his emotions the night before, the tug of arousal had been there. That, at least, was familiar territory. Something he understood. But standing here looking at her he wasn't so sure. He wasn't in control here, either.

It had to do with that look in her eyes he had seen the night before. The same look he could see in them now. Awareness. Yes. Desire. Yes. But where before there had been irritation and annoyance, now there was understanding. It made him very uneasy. Unfortunately, that still didn't stop him from wanting to drag her into his arms and muss up that pretty hairdo.

'Monroe?'

He'd been staring at her blankly for almost a minute, looking dazed. It was so unlike the cool, confident guy she knew. It worried her. She could see then what she'd seen yesterday evening; the confusion in his eyes.

'Right, the painting, sure.' He gave it a quick glance. 'It's too flat.'

She looked past him at it and saw he was exactly right. The oils had been expertly applied but failed to capture the churning magnificence of the sea in full storm mode. 'Gosh, you're right, it's rather cheesy, isn't it?' Jessie turned back to him. 'Monroe, you're staring at me again. What's wrong?'

'Nothing, nothing at—' He stopped, seemed to collect himself. 'I've been invited to a six-year-old's birthday party.'

Jessie grinned. 'You're going to come?'

'Ali didn't give me a choice.' He sounded a little annoyed, she thought, and grinned some more.

'We don't call her the stormtrooper for nothing.'

'It's just that—' he pinned her with his eyes '—I don't know what to get Emmy. For a present, I mean.'

'You don't have to get her anything, Monroe.'

His gaze sharpened. 'Yeah, I do.'

It occurred to Jessie, even if he was down to his last dollar, he would get Emmy a present. And she had once accused him of being a deadbeat. How wrong could a person be?

'There's a lovely little toy shop on Main Street,' she said, feeling guilty, desperate to make amends. 'You're bound to find something perfect in there.'

He gave a furtive glance round, took a step closer. 'No way am I going in there alone.' The words came out on a strained whisper.

'Let me get this straight,' Jessie said, enjoying the look of horror in his eyes. 'A big, bad guy like you is scared of going into a toy shop?'

'Right down to my toes.' He gave a mock shudder. 'When do you get off here?'

Jessie looked at the clock on the gallery's wall. 'In about half an hour.'

'Great, I'll meet you over at the diner. Don't even think about skipping out on me. I'll hunt you down.'

Jessie couldn't imagine why the threat excited her. 'Okay, but you'll owe me.'

'No sweat.' Monroe tapped his finger on her nose. 'See you later, Red.' He sauntered out of the shop.

Jessie grinned, already anticipating an afternoon of toy shopping with the most intriguing, desirable man she'd ever met.

She'd revised her opinion somewhat, ninety frustrating minutes later.

'What is this? A severed head?' Monroe grumbled.

Jessie grabbed the hair and styling doll out of his hands and put it carefully back on the shelf. 'Shh. It's a hair-dressing kit. What about these dolls? She loves them.'

'What the hell?' He stared at the gaudy toys a moment. 'I'm not buying a little kid a doll that looks like a hooker.'

Jessie tried to quell her irritation. After all, it was touching that he would want to get Emmy something really special—but also that he would worry that he might get it wrong. She wondered if he knew how hard he'd fallen for the little girl.

'Don't worry, Monroe.' She laid a hand on his arm. 'We'll get the right gift, even if it takes us all afternoon.'

He dragged his fingers through his hair. 'Thanks. It's important.'

'Yes, it is.' She never would have guessed how important until now.

Jessie studied the row of fussy little boutique shops across the street as they left the toy shop. Her eyes lighted on something at the end of the road, nestled between a cookware emporium and an expensive leatherwear shop. It made a slow smile spread across her face.

'I've just had a fantastic idea.' She grabbed Monroe's hand and pulled him across the street.

'You're a smart lady.' Monroe tucked the small toolbox under his arm. Full of handy little car maintenance accessories, it was just what any budding mechanic could wish for.

'Now all you need is a card and some wrapping paper and you're all set.'

'Great.' The relief in his voice made her smile. 'I owe you big time, Red. How about we grab a beer down by the marina? My treat.'

'That would be lovely.' She looped her arm in his, feeling

more relaxed and comfortable around him than she ever had before. His arm felt solid and warm against hers, the hair on it soft and yet very masculine. The awareness between them was still there, but, having seen him agonise over Emmy's present for over an hour, she didn't find it nearly so threatening. Now would be a good time to bring up the request that had been nagging at her for nearly twenty-four hours. 'Actually, I wanted to ask you a favour, too.'

'Sure. What is it?' He pulled his arm out of hers and rested his hand on the small of her back. Hefting the toolbox under one arm, he drew her close to his side, guiding her through the Saturday shoppers on the raised clapboard sidewalk. His palm seemed to sizzle through the thin silk of her work suit, the possessiveness of his gesture making her feel light-headed.

'I'll tell you when we get to the marina.' Maybe she needed a little Dutch courage after all, Jessie thought.

'Okay, shoot. What was the favour?'

As they settled on the deck of the waterfront bar, two icy beers on the small table between them, Monroe waited for her answer. What could she possibly want from him?

Jessie took a sip of her drink. 'I'd like to see what you've been painting for the last week and a half.'

He paused, the bottle of beer halfway to his lips. 'How do you know about that?' He put the beer back on the table.

'You mentioned it. When we were in the diner that time. Is it supposed to be a secret, then?'

'No.' He picked up a few peanuts from the little dish on the table, cracked them in his palm and then studied them as he removed the shells. 'It's not a secret.'

It wasn't, not really, but he didn't know if he wanted her to see his work. Which was weird. He'd never been bothered about anyone looking at it before. He didn't paint for anyone but himself. He didn't have to justify or prove himself to anyone. But he couldn't help feeling that her opinion would matter to him. What if she hated his stuff? What if she thought it was trash? And why the hell did he care what she thought?

She tilted her head to one side, watching him as he popped the peanuts into his mouth, chewed. 'I only wondered because you've never mentioned it,' she said. 'To Linc or Ali, I mean.'

He swallowed, stretched his legs out under the table, and tried to look relaxed. 'Why would I? It's not important.'

Jessie knew he wasn't telling the truth. His artwork was important to him. He'd been working at it all afternoon and well into the night, every day since he'd arrived.

'All right.' She lingered on the words, could already see the refusal in his eyes. 'If it's not important, you won't mind me seeing them, will you?'

He lifted his bottle again, took a long drag of his beer. 'There's nothing much finished yet.'

He was lying again; she was sure of it. But why? 'Could I look at them when you have?'

He shrugged. 'I guess so, but, like I said, it's no big deal.'

'I'd still love to see them.'

He hitched his shoulders, but the movement was stiff, dismissive.

Jessie turned away and stared at Cranford's famous Tall Ship, standing alone in the bay like the proud sentinel of a bygone era. He'd been deliberately offhand and evasive about his artwork. He didn't want her to see it and the realisation hurt. She thought in the last few days they'd become friends, a little. Yet, it was obvious that he didn't trust her. Not to look at his work anyway. Which must be a very big deal if he would guard it so carefully. Sighing quietly as a small flock of seagulls nearby flew off in a rush, she forced herself to let the hurt go.

She was overreacting, as usual. She liked the easy camaraderie they'd established. If he wasn't ready to show her his work yet, she'd just have to wait.

Turning back, she was discomfited to see him watching her, his beer bottle empty now, the peanuts in the bowl gone.

She plastered a smile on her face. 'Are you coming over for dinner tonight?'

Monroe's brow furrowed. 'Nah, I'll wait for the big birthday bash tomorrow. I don't want to outstay my welcome.' He drained the bottle, pushed his chair back and got up. 'It's getting late. You ought to get back.'

As they paid the bill and left the bustling marina, the sun starting to dip towards the horizon, Jessie wanted to tell Monroe that he couldn't possibly outstay his welcome. That he was family, and family was always welcome.

But she didn't say it. She knew he would reject the personal comment.

As Jessie watched him ride off alone on his Harley and she climbed into the BMW she'd borrowed from Linc that morning, for the first time it occurred to Jessie how lonely Monroe's life was.

He had no one.

How could he survive without family, without any real friends? And was that really the way he wanted it?

She began to wonder as she drove home along the coastal road; was he really as indifferent as he pretended to be? Maybe it wasn't that he didn't want her to see his work. Maybe it wasn't that he didn't want to come over to the house for dinner that night. Maybe he was simply scared to open himself up to something he'd never really known. Family. Approval. Love.

CHAPTER NINE

'HE LOOKS like he's outnumbered. Think I should rescue him?'
Linc's voice in her ear made Jessie jump. She'd been lost in
thought watching Monroe organise a game of tag with five little
girls all clinging to his legs.

Once Ali had strong-armed him into organising the party
games, Jessie had watched him starting to enjoy himself. Emmy
and her little friends obviously adored him. He was a natural with
kids and yet from what he'd said yesterday at the marina it was
clear he wanted to keep the family at arm's length. Couldn't he
see that they could make his life so much richer?

'You know,' Linc continued, 'I think he's beginning to regret
his way with the ladies.' He laughed, the sound low and relaxed
as they watched Monroe pick Emmy up and turn her on her head.
The chorus of squeals that followed made Jessie wince.

'Ali sent me to tell you the food's ready.' Linc glanced down
at Jessie. 'Could you corral the kids over to the pool? I've got a
surprise for Monroe, too. I'm going to go get it. So make sure he
doesn't run off.'

'I'll make sure he's there.' Jessie's eyes followed Linc as he
left the room. A surprise for Monroe. That sounded intriguing.
She clapped her hands over her head but still had to shout to be
heard. 'Emmy, kids. Tea's ready out by the pool. Last one there's
a rotten egg.'

As the little girls ran off in a flurry of frills and shrieks, Monroe
collapsed on the rug.

'Hell, they're like a swarm of locusts,' he groaned.

Jessie smiled down at him. 'You survived.'

'Just about, but it was a close call.' He looked up at her, his arms propping up his long, lean body as he lay back. 'Ali forgot to mention they operate in a pack, like ravenous wolves.'

Jessie laughed, but stopped abruptly when warm, strong fingers gripped her ankle. She gasped when a quick pull had her stumbling on top of him.

'That's better.' His hand shot out and before she knew it she was on top of him, his arms banded around her back, in the middle of the living room floor.

'What do you think you're doing?' She wanted to sound indignant but the heat in his eyes was making her pulse leap like a scared rabbit.

'What I've wanted to do since the last time we did this.' He turned over, taking her with him. Her back was on the floor, his body pressed on top of hers and his lips hot on her mouth before she could blink.

The sudden rush of heat and intensity shocked her. She struggled for a moment, then went still, letting him explore her mouth with his. The flames licking at her belly, making her centre throb, were so shocking and so sudden she couldn't seem to find the will to stop him, or herself. She could feel every inch of him, but most of all his lips. Wet and wonderful on hers. Then he pushed his tongue into her mouth. She gasped and the kiss went deeper, so much deeper it scared her. She struggled against him, pushed him back.

'We have to stop.' Her voice panted out on a breathy sob. 'We're at a children's party.'

He cursed then and moved off her.

She scrambled up. 'I can't believe we did that.'

Her face was so hot it burned. He sat up, draped his arm over one knee and stared up at her. He gave his head a rueful shake. 'Seeing as I've been planning it for over a week, I guess it lacked a bit of finesse.'

'What do you mean planning it?' Why did she suddenly feel totally out of her depth?

He stood up and rested his hands on her hips. She tried to step back, but he held her in place. 'We need to talk, Red.'

* * *

Monroe couldn't believe he'd blown it so badly. But, hell, he'd been watching her for the whole afternoon in that sunny yellow dress. Seeing the way it fitted so demurely, giving a tantalising glimpse of the curves beneath—and he'd wanted to kiss her again ever since that afternoon by the grocery store.

He wasn't a man used to denying his instincts. Damn it, he wasn't a man who usually had to.

So when she'd grinned down at him a moment before, her red hair rioting round her face, that bright, friendly look in her eyes, instinct had taken over. Seeing the way she was staring at him now, flushed but wary, he could have kicked himself.

'What do you want to talk about?' Her voice was tremulous, unsure.

'I want to talk about us.'

'But…' she hesitated '…there is no us.'

'There will be. Don't tell me you don't know it.'

Jessie scrambled about for something coherent to say. She could still feel the pressure of his lips on hers, the solid weight of his body covering her own. And the way he was watching her was making her legs shake and the heat in her belly feel like an inferno. She couldn't seem to get a single coherent thought into her head.

'We can't talk about it now. We have to go cut the cake with Emmy.' She knew it sounded ridiculous, but she couldn't think of anything else to say.

He stroked a finger down her cheek, and then tucked it under her chin, forcing her gaze up to his. 'Sure, Red, but afterwards we talk.'

The bustle and noise of a children's party in full swing helped to calm Jessie's nerves as she stepped out onto the pool terrace.

Five little girls stuffed down biscuits and sweets and chattered away as if their lives depended on it. Linc was pouring out soda into plastic cups like a pro and Ali was busy sticking candles into the cake they had baked that morning.

Monroe gave her hand a quick squeeze, making her heart skip another beat, before walking over to Emmy. Jessie watched as he stroked the little girl's head, leant down to whisper something into her ear. Emmy giggled and handed him a cake off her plate.

'Jessie, great, grab this, will you?' Ali huffed out a breath and handed her the cake—a huge chocolate structure that was supposed to be a fairy-tale castle but looked more like a mound of newly-turned earth. 'Are you okay, Jess? You look a little flushed.'

'I'm fine.' Jessie tried to sound offhand, but as Ali bent down to light the candles, Jessie met Monroe's gaze over her sister's head.

His eyes were intent on hers as he bit slowly into the pink-frosted fairy cake Emmy had handed him. Jessie's heart pounded heavily in her chest. What exactly had she unleashed here?

After a rousing chorus of Happy Birthday and much merriment as Emmy tried three times to blow out her candles, Monroe sauntered back towards Jessie. She couldn't seem to draw her eyes away from him as he came to stand beside her. He flashed her that dimple-cheeked grin but said nothing. She was searching her mind for something to say to him, when Linc's voice boomed out from the other side of the terrace. Thank God, it took Monroe's eyes off her as he turned to listen.

'Now, folks, before we start digging into this—' Linc glanced down at the cake '—very interesting-looking cake—' Ali jabbed her husband in the ribs, making him laugh '—I've got an announcement to make. It so happens Emmy's not the only person in the Latimer household with a birthday this month.'

As Linc reached under the table and drew out a large brightly-wrapped package, Jessie felt Monroe go very still beside her. She turned to look at him. His jaw had gone rigid.

'Turns out—' Linc walked towards Monroe with the package in his arms, smiling '—her uncle's birthday was last Wednesday.' He offered the present to Monroe. 'Better late than never. Happy Birthday, Roe.'

Jessie could hear Emmy and her little friends applauding and doing a spontaneous chorus of Happy Birthday. Ali and the other adults were clapping, Linc was still smiling.

But something was wrong. Monroe made no move to take the gift. He stared down at it, then back at Linc. Embarrassed for both men, Jessie nudged him. 'Take it, Monroe.'

He glanced round at her then. He looked dazed.

'Roe, it's okay,' Linc said softly. Jessie saw his smile fade as he lowered the present.

Ali came up behind her husband and rested her palm on his back.

Monroe still said nothing, still made no move to accept the gift.

Jessie could feel the hollowness inside her. Linc had been so eager, so pleased about the surprise he had planned. It was awful to see him look so dejected. Why didn't Monroe just take the present? Why was he hurting his brother's feelings like this?

She gave Monroe's arm another nudge. 'Take it, Monroe. It's for you.'

Jolted out of whatever trance he seemed to be in, Monroe slowly took the gift out of his brother's hands. But he didn't look at Linc, Jessie saw, her temper rising, he just continued to stare at the prettily-wrapped present.

'I...' Monroe cleared his throat. His Adam's apple jerked, tension snapped in the air around him, tension and something else Jessie couldn't explain. 'I've got to go.'

With a quick nod to Linc, he slung the present under his arm and strode past the dismayed party-goers. He disappeared across the lawn, without looking back once.

Jessie stood dumbstruck. She heard Linc sigh and speak quietly to Ali. 'Hell, that went well.'

Jessie watched Ali rub her husband's back. 'It was the right thing to do, Linc.'

'I don't know,' Linc murmured. 'It was too soon.'

Jessie could see the thin glaze of tears in her sister's eyes as she shook her head, the look of desolation in her brother-in-law's. What were they talking about?

'I can't believe you're being so nice about this,' Jessie said. 'That was rude.'

Both Linc and Ali stared at her. It was as if they'd only just seen her. Jessie's temper and her confusion spiked up another notch. 'I'm going to go and tell him so,' she said. But as she tried to march past them both Ali stopped her.

'Jessie, don't go over there now. Monroe needs time.'

'I don't give a toss what he needs,' Jessie hissed.

Linc had walked off to talk to the other adults, obviously to try and smooth things over. Watching him, Jessie felt her anguish increase at the shoddy way this good, strong man had been treated by his own brother.

'Monroe was totally out of order, Ali. He didn't even say thank you.'

'There are things going on here you don't understand, Jess. This is between Linc and Monroe. You mustn't interfere.'

Jessie bit down on her lip, trying to shore up her temper. What didn't she understand?

'Come on.' Ali gave her a weak smile. 'We need to sort out the party bags. And don't forget Emmy's still got all her presents to open. Will you help me?'

Jessie nodded, but couldn't bring herself to smile back at her sister.

The fact that she didn't understand, that she didn't know what was going on, didn't make her feel any better about what had just happened. It only made her feel angry and insecure. She had come to like Monroe in the last week or so, had come to think she knew him a little. He'd been right when he'd said there was something between them. But it wasn't just passion she felt for him. She had come to care about him. A lot, if she was honest with herself.

The cavalier way he had treated Linc proved to her that she didn't really know him at all. It seemed she had come to care about a man, desire a man, who was a complete stranger. And that frightened her.

Jessie's unhappiness increased as the party bags were handed out and Emmy's presents were opened. The little girl was thrilled with the mechanic's kit Monroe had given her, but threw a small fit when her mother told her she'd have to wait to thank her uncle. Emmy's reaction made Jessie's anger towards Monroe grow. Why had he skulked off like that, without even a thought for Emmy? After spending so long picking out her present yesterday, why hadn't he at least stayed to see it opened? It showed a careless, callous disregard for the little girl's feelings that couldn't be excused.

Finally the last of Emmy's friends and their parents had left the house.

Jessie gritted her teeth and set about tidying up the mess from the party while the rest of the household packed for their trip to New York. By the time she'd finished an hour later, the room was spotless and she'd managed to work up a pretty good head of steam. Monroe had not appeared to apologise.

Jessie helped load up Linc and Ali's people carrier. She mentioned to Ali again that someone should go and talk to Monroe, but Ali simply shook her head as she climbed into the car.

'Let it go, Jess. Don't worry about him.'

It had been on the tip of Jessie's tongue to say she wasn't worried, not about Monroe anyway. But she stopped herself. Ali looked tired, Linc was clearly subdued and they needed to get on their way if they were going to get into the city before midnight.

The minute the car was out of sight, Jessie closed the property's gates and scowled at the garage apartment.

If Ali and Linc were worried about hurting Monroe's feelings—she snorted; as if the man had any feelings—she certainly wasn't. She stalked across the lawn, righteous indignation wrapped around her like a cloak.

She could hear the music blaring from his apartment as she crossed the lawn. Rock music was howling at a decibel level that could make your ears bleed, masking the sound of the cool sea breeze rustling the flowers and tall grass.

It was just another sign of his thoughtlessness. There was no point in knocking, so she marched on in, sailing through on a wave of anger. She shouted his name at the top of her lungs.

And then shouted it two more times before the music shut off.

Her eardrums were still throbbing in time to the rebel chant when Monroe strolled into the room. His chest and feet were bare, his T-shirt hooked through the belt loop of his jeans. Flecks of paint stood out against the dark hair that curled lightly across his chest. The easy grin she had come to expect was gone. His face was hard, his eyes flat and expressionless. He looked savage and intimidating.

'How long have you been here?'

'Long enough.' Jessie clung onto her anger, ignoring the weakness she felt at the sight of him. 'Linc and Ali and Emmy have left, by the way. Just in case you're interested.'

He gave her a dismissive nod. 'If there's nothing else, I'm busy here. I don't have time to chit-chat.'

Jessie sucked in a breath. How dare he talk to her like that?

'You don't say.' She marched up to him, stabbed a finger into his chest. 'You should have come and said goodbye. You should have apologised to Linc. You hurt him.'

Something flashed into his eyes at the mention of his brother's name. But then his face went hard again. He grabbed onto her finger, held it away from him, but his voice remained calm. 'You don't want to be around me right now. I'm not feeling civilised.'

She heard the menace in his words and pulled her finger free. She didn't know this man at all. He looked dangerous. He was breathing heavily as if he'd been running, the firm bronzed skin of his chest glistened with sweat, but his eyes were so remote it was frightening.

She took a step back. 'What happened by the pool? Why was it so hard for you to take the gift?'

Suddenly, she wanted desperately to know, to understand. Where was the man she'd come to care for?

'Just because we've shared a few hot kisses…' he gave her a slow, deliberate once-over '…just because I'd like to see you naked, doesn't mean you're my shrink.'

He was trying to upset her. With a flash of insight she saw that he wanted her to run. 'Why are you being deliberately cruel? It's not like you.'

'You don't know what I'm like.'

Something swirled into his eyes as he turned away. Unhappiness? Pain? Was he hurting, too?

'Monroe, what is it?' She walked up behind him. He stood in front of the window, the muscles of his back and shoulders rigid.

'I'm warning you, Jessie. You need to get out of here.'

He didn't look round. She studied the thin white scars that marred the smooth, bronzed skin. Reaching up, she hesitated a moment and then stroked her fingers down his spine.

He shot round. 'Don't touch me.'

She could see his eyes clearly now. Desperation and confusion burned in the blue depths.

'Tell me. What is it? Why was it so hard for you to take Linc's present?'

'I didn't know how.' He shouted the words, fisted his hands in frustration and thrust them into his pockets. 'I've never been given a birthday gift before in my whole damn life.'

CHAPTER TEN

ANGER at himself churned like molten lava in Monroe's gut. Anger and a desire that he was struggling real hard to ignore.

He'd been raw, ragged with emotions he'd never felt before ever since Linc had handed him the birthday gift two hours ago. And guilt was right slam-bang at the top of the list.

He'd played them all, like an orchestra. He'd done a few odd jobs, befriended the little girl and managed to con them all into thinking he was a good guy—Emmy, Linc, Ali and most of all, Jessie.

Since he'd got out of prison, Monroe's life had been nomadic. It was the way he liked it. Women had come and gone, friendships had been shallow and fleeting. He didn't want it to be any different.

But when Linc had held the present out to him, the sparkly wrapping paper glinting in the sunshine, all those foolish old feelings of wanting to have a place to belong had come flooding back. He'd realised in a rush that they'd all accepted him into their home, into their hearts. The yearning that had gripped him at the thought, the desperate need to be accepted, had stunned him. But worse had been the knowledge that he could never have a place here.

Because he wasn't a good guy, not really.

He was a user. He used people and moved on. That way he didn't have to be bothered by anyone but himself.

He'd taken Linc's gift in a daze of confusion and pain. He'd stormed back to the apartment, turned up the stereo to blast level and painted like a madman. But the storm of emotions had continued to churn inside him. And when Jessie had shown up, the only thing he could think was he had to make her run before he took something he could never give back.

She was beautiful, fresh, impulsive and honest. No wonder he wanted her so badly; she was all the things he wasn't.

Looking down at her, seeing the concern in her eyes as she absorbed what he'd said about the present, he wanted to take her so badly, claim her so badly, it hurt.

'Why did you never have a birthday gift before?' she asked gently.

He could hear the compassion and it crucified him. He shrugged. 'I don't live like that. All neat and pretty.'

He turned, stared blankly out the window at the gathering dusk, the darkening red of sunset mirroring his own shadowed thoughts. He couldn't look at her and tell her the truth. 'I do what I want, when I want. I don't have a family. I don't need one. Nobody's going to tie me down. That's the way I like it.'

Jessie could hear the defiance, the desperation in his words. She had been right, was all she could think. He was lonely and he was scared.

No wonder he hadn't been able to take Linc's present. It had meant something to him he didn't understand. It meant love and trust and affection. All things he'd spent most of his life without. He was always so sure of himself, so cocky. But beneath that was a good, caring man who needed things that he seemed determined to deny himself.

Jessie had a huge well of love inside her that she wanted to give to someone. And here was a man who needed it. She wouldn't ask herself why Monroe denied love, denied family. It was enough for now to know he needed her and she needed him.

She'd been falling in love all along—and now she knew why.

He was the one she'd been waiting for. He was everything she'd ever wanted, standing there before her. So handsome, so vulnerable and so confused. Taking the next step now was all that mattered. The rest of it would sort itself out in time.

'Everybody needs family, Monroe,' she said softly.

He swung around, his eyes fixed on hers. 'Damn it. Don't you get it? I used you. I saw something I wanted, so I went after it.' His voice was rough with self-loathing. 'You heard what I said when I jumped you at the party. I've been planning this all along.

Getting you to like me. Getting you to trust me. It was all just a damn game so I could get you into bed.'

She laughed, the mix of arousal and excitement making her light-headed. He wanted her. 'If that was the plan, you seem to be mucking it up a bit now.'

'What?' His mouth dropped open.

She stepped forward, drew her hands up his chest, wrapped her fingers around his neck. He smelt wonderful—linseed oil, turpentine and the musky smell of man. He felt even better. The hard, rigid muscles of his chest quivered against her breasts, as if he were a racehorse, ready to leap out of a starting gate. She had the power. For the first time, she was the one in control.

'You know, Monroe.' Her voice came out on a soft purr; she heard him swallow. 'It was really nice of you to do all the work, up to this point.' She caressed the back of his neck, threading her fingers through the soft hair of his nape.

He shuddered.

'But it looks like I'm going to have to take over now,' she said.

He pulled her into his arms, forcing her hard against him. 'You're playing with dynamite, Red. I'm no saint.' Slowly, he drew his palms up her sides, his thumbs caressing the swell of her breasts through the linen of her dress. 'If you keep on going the way you are, I'm going to have you and to hell with the consequences.'

She drew in a sharp breath at the harsh demand on his face. The fire in his eyes made her knees go to jelly, but she kept her voice steady. 'Promises, promises.'

The teasing words were barely out before his lips cut her off. He feasted on her mouth, thrusting his tongue in as his hands came up to fist in her hair. She began to shake, her breath gushing out when he lifted his head.

'Are you sure about this?' he rasped in her ear, his voice low and barely controlled. 'You've got to be sure.' His lips skidded up her neck as he spoke.

'I'm positive,' she murmured.

His lips covered hers again. His tongue probed, demanding entry. Her mouth opened, allowing him to explore her, to devastate her.

He stopped, rested his forehead on hers. 'I want to look at you, Red.'

His fingers came up in a brief caress, then he tugged the straps off her shoulders, pushed the dress down to her waist. She pulled her arms free.

Nudging the lacy cup of her bra down, he bent his head to watch as he exposed her breast. Fire flared in her belly, flooding between her thighs. His lips, hot and insatiable, closed over the swollen peak, suckled strongly. Her breath caught as the arrow of lust shot down to her centre.

Fumbling, he released the clasp, pulled the bra off. He stood back, holding her away from him. She flushed as his eyes devoured her body, naked from the waist.

'You're beautiful, Red,' he murmured. He cupped the ripe breast in callused palms, rubbed his thumbs over the engorged nipples. She went lax under his stroking hands. The heat was so intense now, she felt she might faint.

He pulled the dress down the rest of the way, taking her hand as she stepped free on teetering legs. He hooked his finger in the thin cotton of her panties and ripped them off. She gasped, totally exposed before him, drifting beyond pleasure to panic.

Lifting her limp body high in his arms, he stalked to the sofa, laid her down. She watched him, dazed and unsure, as he stripped off his jeans. He seemed savage, overwhelming all of a sudden. What had she done?

The muscles of his chest heaved from his staggered breathing. His arousal jutted out. He looked magnificent, like a powerful male animal.

She wanted to cover herself, but seemed powerless to do anything, enthralled by the sight of him as he knelt beside her. He stroked his fingers across her belly, making her jump as he reached lower and gently probed the folds of her sex. She could feel how wet she was as his thumb glided over the nub he exposed. She shuddered violently and cried out.

'I'm sorry, Red. I can't wait.' He lay on top of her, his weight making her sink into the soft cushions. He grasped her hips, his eyes harsh on her face, and she felt trapped beneath him. Still she was dazed, detached, as he positioned himself, probed and then thrust within. She cried out, the shocking fullness and discomfort hurling her out of the strange trance and slamming her hard into reality.

She grabbed at his shoulders, pushed frantically. 'Stop it. It hurts,' she cried out.

He reared back.

She could see the surprise and confusion in his eyes and the rigid control as his arms tensed at her sides.

'What's wrong?' He pulled out of her, cupped her face in unsteady hands. She could see the bitter regret in his face and she shattered—the pent-up emotions of long years of inadequacy and denial bursting out.

'I can't do this. I'm no good at it.' She began to shake, raw with humiliation. The misery engulfed her. Why had she thought that with him it might work? For a while, as they'd kissed and caressed it had been so wonderful. She'd been spun up in a whirlwind of passion and excitement. But then, it had been dragged away. She'd failed, as always.

He held her gently, drawing her into his arms, settling her close.

'Shh. Don't cry. I rushed you. I went too damn fast. It's my fault.'

'It's not.' She snuffled, determined to tell him the truth. 'I'm rubbish at this. I've been told I'm frigid.'

She wanted to get up, get away. But his arms tightened around her, holding her in place.

'Please, I have to go.' She could hear the pathetic whimper in her voice and despised herself for it.

She couldn't look at him. Couldn't bear to see the disappointment in his eyes, or, worse, the pity. But then he tucked his finger under her chin, forced her face up to his.

'Don't go, Red.' There was no pity, just concern. He touched his lips to hers, the kiss so gentle it was like a whisper. 'Who's the dumb bastard who said you were frigid?'

'Toby. His name was Toby Collins.'

'Toby, huh?' He pushed the hair from her brow, brushed it back carefully as he met her eyes. Then his own went hard with anger. 'I'd like to get Toby Collins and string him up by his nuts.'

'Oh!' What else was there to say?

He looked so fierce and forbidding she almost felt sorry for her former fiancé. If Toby hadn't been on the other side of the Atlantic, his nuts would surely be in grave danger.

Monroe drew her closer. 'But seeing as Toby and his pea-sized nuts aren't here right now, we're gonna have to undo the damage he did instead.'

'What do you mean?' she asked, wary of the determination in his voice.

'You're not frigid. And we're going to prove it.'

She tensed in his arms, painfully aware of his nakedness and her own.

'I don't…' She paused. 'That's really not necessary.'

'Oh, yeah, it is.' He dipped his head, took her lips in a slow, tender kiss.

The low throbbing in her belly seemed to come from nowhere. But she drew back, flushed but horribly unsure of herself. 'I don't think I can, Monroe.'

He trailed a finger down across her breast, watching it intently as he circled the peak.

'You can do it.' He glanced up, dazzled her with that easy, confident grin she knew so well. 'If you're treated with the proper care and attention.'

His fingertip toyed with her nipple. A breath she hadn't realised she'd been holding gushed out. She glanced down at him hard against her thigh. Her breath caught in her throat; he was still fully aroused and he looked enormous.

His grin spread as her shocked gaze met his. 'We were so close before. We're going to take it real slow and easy this time and do it right.'

He levered himself up, got off the couch and pulled her up with him. Dumping the two large cushions onto the floor, he knelt on them and then tugged her down beside him. 'Lie down.'

She did as she was told, confused and wary, feeling hideously exposed, like an offering on a sacrificial altar, as he lay down next to her.

'Don't look so worried.' He kissed her. 'The only rules are, you don't think and you don't touch. All right?'

'Okay.'

Slowly, carefully, he began to stroke his fingers down the length of her. He seemed to take for ever. At first, she felt foolish, inadequate, but when his touch swept the underside of her breast, she shuddered. His fingers trailed down her arms next, catching the soft skin inside her elbow, and she gasped. Then he found the sensitive place behind her knee as he drew her legs up.

Her centre throbbed, insistent and intense. He followed his hands with his lips and when she tried all she could think of was where he would go next. Anticipation, then delight. The process was slow, delicious torture as his tongue delved and dipped, stroked and slid across her heated flesh.

She had to touch him. But when his lips closed over her nipple and she tried to grab his head, he pulled back. Capturing her wrists in one hand, he held them above her head. 'No touching. Remember?'

'Please, I want to feel you, too.' The words came out on a sob as she strained against him, but he simply shook his head and held her in place.

It seemed he caressed her breasts for ever. Lathing the sensitive tips and then blowing softly, making them pucker fiercely before his appreciative gaze. Making her writhe against his controlling hands.

She panted, all thoughts flown from her head but the unbearable heat, the intense pleasure at her core. Her heart raced so fast, it would surely explode. The burning between her thighs was so intense she couldn't draw breath. He released her wrists to circle the soft skin of her inner thighs. At last, he was going to touch her there, where she needed him most. But still his fingers teased, stroking the soft curls at the juncture. Finally, he probed within. The touch was barely there, but her sigh choked out on a sob. Then he stroked again, pushing the folds back, watching her face. His eyes held hers as she sobbed again. She was clinging to the edge of a desperate precipice. He was there now, right at the heart of the heat, making it burn.

'I… Please, don't stop.' She didn't know what she was begging for, but saw his slow grin, the blaze of desire in his eyes.

'Let it go, Red.'

He purred the words as she shot over the edge. Everything inside her released, crashed down and then exploded into a million tiny, glittering pieces. She could hear herself, a thousand miles away, cry out on a shattered moan.

'Come on, baby, we're not through yet.'

She was still shivering, dazed by the aftermath of passion as he reared above her. He held her legs apart and settled between them. Angling her hips up with firm hands, he probed at her entrance and then pushed his rigid sex within in one long, slow, shocking thrust.

The fullness was unbearable. She felt stretched, impaled. But where before there had been pain, now there was only the sure, unstoppable rush of pleasure. She sobbed as passion slammed back into her full force, like a runaway train, hard and fast and out of control.

'Look at me, Red. I want to see you do it again.' His voice was low, thick with desire. Her eyes fixed on his face. He looked so gorgeous at that moment. The inferno built inside her with each powerful thrust.

She soared over this time, falling free as they shouted out their release together.

CHAPTER ELEVEN

'Wow!' Jessie stroked Monroe's back. She loved the solid feel of him on top of her, his ragged breathing echoing her own.

He grunted and lifted himself up on his elbows. 'Am I crushing you?'

'Yes.' She sighed, enjoying the flushed look on his face. She'd done that to him, she thought, and welcomed the rush of female power. 'But don't go.' She hugged him. 'I like it.'

He smiled, but eased away. Turning on his side, he tugged her to him with one arm. The cushions had fallen apart in their frenzy, leaving them in a dip between the two. He tucked a tendril of her flyaway hair behind her ear. 'You're looking kinda smug, Red.'

'I am?' She laughed, the sound girlish. His eyes flared with arousal. 'That was…' She paused. How should she say this, without sounding ridiculous? 'That was unbelievable. I mean, I never… I never had the foggiest…' She stumbled to a halt, realising his grin had widened. She was making an idiot of herself.

He stroked a finger slowly across her midriff. The feel of it, warm and lazy, made her shiver. 'The foggiest?' He chuckled. 'Is that your cute English way of saying this was your first time?'

'No, of course not. I'm not a virgin. Don't be ridiculous. I'm twenty-six years old.' She wanted to sound indignant, but it was hard with his fingers trailing down to the red curls at her core.

'But that was your first orgasm, right?' Now who sounded smug?

'Okay, yes, it was.' She felt foolish, now, foolish but unbearably needy as his fingers stopped circling and he looked at her.

Pride, fierce and possessive, blazed in his eyes. 'Well, it sure as hell won't be your last.' He patted her bottom. 'You can bet on that.' His lips quirked as he started to rise.

She reached for him. 'Don't go.'

'Don't worry, I'll be back.' He knelt beside her. 'You know, Red, you make one hell of a picture.'

She crossed her arms over her chest, feeling shy, but he drew her hands away. He kissed both her palms in turn. The gesture was so gentle, so loving, it made her heart swell.

He stood up. 'I'll go get something to clean you up.'

As he headed for the bathroom, his words registered. She felt it then, the stickiness between her thighs. She bolted upright.

'Monroe.' He turned, naked and beautiful, and looked back at her. 'I…' Her face burned. 'We didn't use a condom.'

Monroe could see the fear in Jessie's eyes. Walking back, he squatted beside her, touched the side of her face.

'Don't panic, Red. I don't have any nasty diseases, I swear. This is the first time I haven't been properly dressed for the party since I was fourteen.' It occurred to him that he hadn't even thought about using a condom.

'I didn't even think of that.' Jessie's face went an even brighter shade of red. 'I've never done it before without protection either. You know, in case you were worried about me.'

He drew his finger slowly down her cheek, his lips curved.

'That's good,' he said, feeling the swell of pride and possessiveness.

How could she be so untouched and so arousing at the same time? He realised he was starting to stir again. He stood up and reached for the jockeys still tucked into his jeans. He didn't want to scare her. But as he took a step back towards the bathroom she got up and touched his arm.

'Monroe, it's not just, well…' she swallowed audibly '…it's not just communicable diseases. I'm not on the pill. I could get pregnant.'

Jessie was so embarrassed she wanted to die on the spot. One minute she'd been the flame-haired seductress she'd always wanted to be and the next a silly schoolgirl. Why hadn't she told him she wasn't on the pill? She was such a complete idiot.

He went very still and stared at her for what seemed like an eternity. Was he annoyed? she wondered. But he didn't look annoyed. It was strange, but for a moment she thought he looked sad. Then he simply shook his head.

'Come here.' Holding her hand, he threw one of the cushions back onto the sofa, sat on it and pulled her into his lap. Tugging the throw rug off the back, he wrapped it carefully around her. 'When's your next period due?' he asked in a quiet voice.

'Not for a while. I finished one less than a week ago.'

'I don't think there's much reason to worry, then. You only usually get pregnant in the middle of your cycle.' He pulled the throw rug to one side, laid a warm palm on her belly and rubbed slowly. When he looked up, his smile was warm, but she could still see that faraway look in his eyes. 'We'll make sure we use protection from now on. Okay?'

She chewed her lip. 'You're not annoyed with me—for not saying something sooner, I mean?'

He lifted his hand, held her chin and kissed her. His lips were light and tender on hers. 'I should have asked and I didn't. I guess we're both guilty of getting carried away.' He lifted her off his lap. He leaned down and gave her a gentle kiss on the forehead and then a long, slow kiss on the lips.

He was so gentle she felt herself getting aroused again. She could see from his boxers that he was aroused, too. She pulled him towards her.

'Don't tempt me, Red.'

'Oh, Monroe.' She put her palm on his cheek.

He put his hand over hers, drew it down. 'We can wait till tomorrow for the next round. Anyhow, I need to get some condoms, remember?'

Although Monroe was desperate for her, no way was he going to take her to bed again so soon. He'd seen the heart-melting look in her eyes after they'd made love. Didn't doubt that she probably thought she was falling in love with him. She was young and naïve and unbearably sweet. A romantic to the core. He was older, much more cynical and had never had a romantic moment in his life. Thank heaven.

He knew that great sex, no, *fantastic* sex, was all he could give her. So they'd keep things light and simple and they'd both have a good time. He felt okay with it, knowing that he could give her something she'd never had before. That first orgasm was just the start, for both of them. He wouldn't think about the future because they didn't have one.

'I better get dressed.' Jessie stood up, struggling with the throw. Why did she suddenly feel as if there was a distance between them that hadn't been there before? 'I should go.'

'No, you don't.' He swung her up into his arms.

She grabbed for his shoulders and the throw fell away, exposing her to the waist.

'What are you doing?' She tried to cling on and pull the throw back up.

'Forget about that.' He tightened his arms. 'I want you naked in my bed tonight.' He sniffed at her hair. 'God, you smell fantastic. No way you're going anywhere tonight.'

She was clinging onto his neck now, his chest hair brushing unbearably against the swollen, sensitive peaks of her breasts. 'But I thought we weren't going to do it again.'

He laughed, the sound rough and rueful. 'Red, you've got so much to learn.' He wiggled his brows, lasciviously. 'Wouldn't you know it? I guess I'm gonna have to teach you.'

He didn't sound remotely put out about it.

Kicking the throw rug away, he sauntered through into the bedroom with her. Bumping the door closed, he whirled her round into the room.

Jessie saw the bed first, a large mattress on the floor, the bed sheets strewn across it, but as he knelt down to dump her on it her head fell back and she caught a glimpse of the blaze of colours over his shoulder.

'Oh, my goodness, Monroe.' She scrambled out of his arms and rushed over to the canvases stacked against the wall.

They were strong, bold, striking images. People's faces, some tender, some touching, others unbearably sad and strong. Stunning landscapes of vibrancy and life. Ugly urban places that had a haunting beauty. Each one of his subjects leapt off the canvas in its own distinct way. His use of colour, of light, of contrast was vivid and demanding, as if he had drawn the emotion out with the paint. She turned back to him, tears forming in her eyes. He stood next to the mattress, watching her, his eyes carefully blank.

'That bad, huh?'

'Monroe.' Walking to him, she placed her palms on his cheeks, searched his face. 'They're incredible. You have an amazing talent.'

'You like them?'

'Are you joking? I don't like them. I love them. They're phenomenal.' She turned, ran back, picked up a small square canvas of a woman and a girl, standing by a gas pump. The girl, who looked little more than a child, was heavily pregnant. Her eyes shone with bitterness and defiance. The paint strokes were rough, the fierce strength elemental on the girl's face.

As she studied it Jessie felt her own emotions well up inside her. 'You've captured her so perfectly. Who was she?'

'Hey.' Walking up behind her, he scooped the tear off Jessie's cheek, laid a hand on her shoulder. 'Don't cry, Jess. The guy responsible stuck by her and so did her mom. She did okay.'

Jessie put the canvas back against the wall, turned to him. 'I'm not crying because of her. She looks tough enough to wrestle an ox. I'm crying because of your art, Monroe. It's so exquisite.'

He looked taken aback. 'You like them that much?'

Monroe pulled her into his arms, the surge of pride inside him so huge it was choking him. No one had ever said something to him that could have meant more. This was better than when she'd had her first orgasm in his arms and that had been pretty damned overwhelming.

'It's only a hobby,' he said, inhaling the fresh, flowery scent of her hair.

She drew back. 'Don't lie.' She took another long look at his paintings. When she turned back, her eyes were full of wonder. His knees felt shaky.

'That's not a hobby,' she said softly. 'That's a passion.'

CHAPTER TWELVE

'JESSIE, dear, your young man's outside.'

Jessie's stomach did a little flip as Mrs Bennett walked into the gallery's tiny office. The leap of joy was something she'd got used to in the last few days.

'He's only a few minutes early,' her boss continued as she put the sales invoices down on Jessie's desk. 'You can go now if you like.'

'Thank you, Mrs Bennett.' Jessie tapped the shutdown button on the desktop computer, grabbed her bag from under the desk and ran out.

Monroe stood outside the gallery's main doors. He looked tall and slightly tense through the glass. Her young man. Wasn't that the most wonderful phrase in the whole wide world?

They'd been together now for four whole days and she felt as if her heart were going to burst in her chest at the sight of him. Had she ever been happier in her life?

The sex, of course, was fabulous. The man made love like a god. She'd never experienced anything like it before. Toby had always treated foreplay like a chore. Maybe that was why she'd never been able to relax, enjoy it. Monroe seemed to know instinctively what to do to make her forget everything except the touch, the feel of him.

But it wasn't Monroe's lovemaking skills that had dazzled her, had lifted her onto a cloud of such intense pleasure and contentment. It was the companionship. They made love every morning and then they would have breakfast in his apartment before he took her to work on the Harley. He'd be waiting outside to pick her up when she got off at noon and then they'd drive like mad things straight back to the apartment and make long, lazy love together all afternoon and most of the evening.

And yesterday, he'd brought her flowers, for goodness' sake. A small bunch of wildflowers he'd said he'd spotted on the way in to town. His obvious embarrassment, when he'd thrust them at her, the delicate blooms wilting in the heat, had only made the gesture more wonderful. It was so romantic.

Thinking about their tempestuous lovemaking by the pool afterwards made Jessie's heartbeat throb heavily and the flush hit her cheeks as she pushed open the door of the gallery.

'Monroe!' She flung her hands around his neck, making him almost drop the grocery sack in his arms.

'Watch it, Red. This is our lunch.'

She pressed her lips to his. 'I'm too happy to see you to care about food.'

The grin spread slowly across his face. 'Is that right?' He slung the sack under his arm, put one hand around her waist and pulled her closer. 'Let's do that again.'

The kiss was long and heated this time. 'Mmm.' He licked his lips. 'Damn it, there you go tempting me again. You'll make me forget.'

'Forget what?'

'Come on. The Harley's round the back.' He gripped her hand, pulled her behind him down the small alleyway that led to the customer car park.

'Are we going home?' She certainly hoped so.

'No way.' He shot her a quick grin, but carried on walking, forcing Jessie to jog to keep up with his long strides. 'You'll just end up jumping me again.'

'Yes, please.'

'Who knew you sweet little English girls could be so damned insatiable?'

'Well, really.' Jessie laughed. 'Who knew you Yankee guys would get knackered so quickly?'

'Knackered!' He stopped in front of the Harley, dumped the grocery sack on the bike seat and put his hands on her hips. He placed a light kiss on her lips, his eyes challenging. 'You wanna bet on that?'

'I certainly do.' She drew her arms up, threaded her fingers through the soft, shaggy gold-streaked hair that she adored. 'Still think you can handle me?'

His hands slid around to her bottom, massaging the flesh through the thin fabric of the cotton trouser suit she wore. 'If it's a matter of my Yankee honour.' He dipped his head, took her lips in a hot, demanding kiss.

She drew back, breathless. 'You win, Yankee boy.'

He gave her bottom one more quick squeeze and then let her go. 'Hell, I guess that means I don't get to ravish you, right?'

'You can't have it both ways, buster,' she said, lifting a coquettish eyebrow.

He sighed, pulled her helmet out of the bike's saddlebags and handed it to her. 'Mount up. We're going on a picnic.'

The streets of Cranford were clogged with tourists. Monroe had to ease the bike down Main Street, threading through the crowds of people heading to the town's beach. The old-fashioned clapboard sidewalks were overflowing, spilling tourists into the road like so much flotsam. The midday sun was a killer, scorching bare flesh and making children cranky and unmanageable.

Monroe didn't mind the delay a bit. He could feel Jessie's arms tight around his waist, her thighs pressed against his hips. As much as he would have loved to head straight home, he forced himself not to.

He'd gorged on her the last four days. But it seemed the more of her he had, the more he needed. The way she responded to him was like a fire in his blood, making him want more all the time, making him take more. He knew he'd exhausted her last night—and himself.

He'd slept like a log.

Ever since prison he'd had trouble getting to sleep. Not any more, it seemed. With her in his arms, snuggled against him in the darkness, the stir of passion still flowing through him, he'd drifted off like a baby.

He'd decided on the way to town that this afternoon was going to be different. He was going to prove he could keep his hands off her.

He'd stopped by the grocery store on his way into the gallery and picked up some stuff for lunch. He knew of a nice little spot

at Montauk Point that shouldn't be too crowded, but there would
be enough people about to stop him getting any ideas. Not that
he needed them there, of course; he could keep his hands off her
if he had to.

As the bike finally cruised past the town limits he revved his
hand on the throttle. As they shot down Sunrise Highway, he
couldn't ignore the thrill that surged through him as Jessie's arms
tightened around his waist.

Jessie could see the lighthouse, tall and solitary at the end of the
point, as the sea breeze whipped at her face. She clung onto Monroe
as the bike angled down to the left, along a narrow strip of path that
led to a small spray of sand hugging the Point's leeward side. A few
tourists had been milling about up top, but once Monroe brought
the bike to a stop at the edge of the sand she couldn't see anyone.

Could Monroe have found anywhere more romantic for their
picnic? Maybe missing their afternoon lovemaking session
wouldn't be so terrible after all.

He took her hand as they walked onto the sand. The bracken
bushes provided some handy shade from the noon sun as he
spread a thin blanket on the ground, and dropped the brown
paper sack onto it.

Jessie took off her jacket, the lacy camisole beneath fluttered
in the breeze and cooled her heated flesh. Sitting down, she toed
off her sandals and reached for the bag.

'I certainly hope we've got something more inspired than sandwiches in here,' she said. 'I'm starving.'

'You know what?' He sank down onto the blanket next to her
and grabbed the grocery sack. 'She who doesn't buy doesn't get
to belly-ache about what's in the bag.'

'What are those—Latimer house rules?' Jessie's lips curved as
she watched him pull an assortment of ready-made salads and a
large foil bag out of the sack.

'Yeah,' he said as he brought out a chilled bottle of wine with
a flourish. 'Now who's griping?'

'Not me,' she replied.

He up-ended the sack and paper plates, plastic cups, napkins,
forks and a bottle opener dropped onto the blanket.

'You thought of everything. I'm impressed.' Jessie tried to sound contrite but was enjoying the moment too much. He looked so pleased with himself. Like a little boy who'd just got straight As for the first time.

As he concentrated on opening the wine, Jessie leant forward on her knees and placed her hands on his shoulder. When his head came up, she put her lips on his. The kiss was a whisper, full of the love blossoming inside her.

He dropped the wine, fisted his fingers in her hair. Dragging her mouth across his, he plundered. The kiss shot to scorching, but only for a moment. When he released her, his face was dark with arousal, and something else, something she wasn't sure of.

He scooped up the bottle of wine. 'Don't get carried away, Red. We haven't tasted it yet.'

Jessie forced herself to ignore the stab of regret. Why hadn't he carried on kissing her? Don't be a ninny. Of course he didn't want to take things any further—they were on a public beach. Anyone might see them. But she couldn't quite shake the feeling that he had withdrawn for some other reason.

She turned round on the blanket, stared out at the waves gently lapping against the shore. She could hear the screech of seagulls overhead, see the tip of the lighthouse in the distance over the long grass and bracken that edged the bluff.

'Here you go, Red.' He nudged her arm. She turned and took the plastic cup. He tapped it with his own. 'Here's to sand in your potato salad.'

Jessie forced her lips to curve. 'Here's to guys who know how to pack a picnic.'

Monroe took a long gulp of the light, fresh white wine. It tasted pretty good, but did nothing to calm the fire inside him.

She had wanted to continue the embrace, had looked disappointed when he'd pulled his mouth away. That fact and the memory of her warm and willing in his arms was making the need claw in his gut like an angry dog. He screwed the plastic glass down into the sand and started pulling the wrapper off the plates.

He'd brought her here to have a nice sensible lunch, not climb all over her again as soon as they got here. He refused to feel bad about it. Even though the confusion in her eyes and the surge of blood to his groin made it damn near impossible not to drag her across his lap right now and…

Jessie opened the salads, searched for something to say as she arranged them on the blanket. 'Ali called the gallery today.'

'How are they doing?'

'Ali's exhausted. I don't think she's left the penthouse much.'

'The heat's a bitch in Manhattan in August.' Monroe ladled some potato salad onto her plate, then his.

'Emmy's having a great time, though. Linc took her to the Bronx Zoo yesterday.' Jessie laughed, remembering the conversation with her sister that morning. 'She said Linc was so shattered when they got back he could hardly string together a coherent sentence.'

Monroe chuckled. 'I bet Emmy was still chattering away like a little magpie. The poor guy.' Tearing open the foil sack, he put a piece of fried chicken on Jessie's plate. 'Did you say anything to Ali about us?'

Jessie glanced up, watched him lick his fingers. 'No, I didn't.' Was that relief she saw flash in his eyes? No, she was being silly, paranoid. 'Ali wouldn't be all that surprised, though.'

'Why?'

Jessie wished she hadn't blurted that out. How did she explain the statement without sounding pathetic?

'It's just…' She looked down at her plate, concentrated on forking up the potato salad. 'I used to have a pretty massive crush on Linc when they were first married.'

'You're kidding me?'

She looked up. He put his fork down on his plate. He was watching her, his expression unreadable.

'It's silly really. It was just a stupid schoolgirl's fantasy.'

He dumped the plate down on the blanket. 'What kind of schoolgirl's fantasy, exactly?'

'Not that kind of fantasy, you numbskull.' Was he jealous? It was so ridiculous it was almost sweet. If she hadn't felt like a complete fool for bringing up this whole business, she might have been flattered. 'It took me a while to realise it, but it wasn't Linc I fancied. Well, not much anyway. It was what he represented.'

* * *

'And what was that?' Monroe didn't even know why he was asking the question. He didn't want the answer.

Jessie huffed out a breath, put her own plate down. 'He adored Ali. It was obvious whenever they were together that they adored each other. And then, about a month after they announced they were getting married, they told us that Ali was expecting a baby.' Jessie picked up her fork, toyed with her food. 'Of course, it was wonderful news. We were all so excited.'

Monroe wasn't convinced. He could see the misery in her eyes at the memory. 'You sure about that?'

'A part of me was,' she said, so quietly he almost couldn't hear her over the churn of the sea. 'But a part of me was pea-green with envy.'

'Because she was having Linc's kid?' He really didn't want to hear the answer to this one.

'No,' she said.

The knot of tension in his shoulders released.

'Because she had this perfect life,' Jessie continued. 'Marriage to a gorgeous man who worshipped her. When Emmy arrived, a beautiful daughter.' Jessie shook her head, her eyes downcast. 'I was a stupid, selfish, silly little girl who wanted what she had without having to work for it.'

'Red.' He reached out, stroked his hand down her arm. 'Don't be so damn hard on yourself. You were only a kid at the time.'

'I was old enough to know better. And I didn't really get over it until after Toby.'

'Toby.' Monroe felt his shoulders tighten again. 'The dumb bastard who couldn't give you an orgasm?'

Jessie laughed, breaking the tension at last. 'Yes, that would be Toby.'

'How long were you guys together?' Funny, but he didn't feel nearly as threatened by her relationship with her ex-boyfriend as he did by her teenage crush on his brother.

'Two years.' She sighed, picked up her plate again. 'Two very long years.'

'Two years without an orgasm. No wonder they felt long. You'd have to be some kind of a nun not to be mad about that.'

'If I had known what I was missing, I'd have walked out on him in about two seconds.' Jessie started to laugh.

Monroe smiled back at her. No, he didn't feel remotely threatened by Toby the jerk.

'But then again,' Jessie said, sobering, 'Toby's abilities in bed weren't why I agreed to marry him.'

'You were going to marry the guy? What the hell for?'

Jessie gave a small smile. 'Well, because he asked me, for one thing. And because he told me he wanted to have children, make a home. For a while there, I persuaded myself he was my dream come true.'

Monroe felt the mouthful of potato salad he'd eaten turn over in his stomach. 'That's your dream? A home, kids?'

Jessie frowned. He looked stunned. No, not stunned, he looked horrified. Just for a moment, before he looked away.

'Well, yes. Sort of. But not right now.'

Was he scared she was going to ask him to marry her or something? While it was lowering to know the question might put that devastated look in his eyes, even she wasn't that much of a romantic fool. They'd only been together for four days, for goodness' sake.

'Monroe, you don't have to look so worried. I'm not picking out the bridesmaids' dresses yet. I learned my lesson with Toby. If I do settle down, it'll be when the time's right with the right person.' She was not going to make a fool of herself over that fantasy again.

He lifted up the wine. 'Put up your glass, Red.'

She lifted the plastic cup, trying to figure out what she could see in his eyes as he splashed some more wine into it.

'Let's drink to dreams, then.' He put down the bottle, picked up his own cup and shot her that heart-breaking grin. 'And not letting them get in the way of good sex.'

Jessie smiled, tapped her cup to his. 'Now that, I can drink to.'

Monroe swallowed the wine, but it tasted like acid on his tongue. Why the hell did he care that he could never be her dream man? That he could never make her dreams come true. He wasn't in the business of dreaming. Reality was hard enough.

CHAPTER THIRTEEN

'FLIP over. I've been fantasising about putting sunscreen on that back since we got here.'

Jessie smiled at the low rumble of Monroe's voice. Lying on the small stretch of private beach next to Linc and Ali's property, she could feel the familiar warmth that had nothing to do with the early-morning sunshine.

She sat up, dipped her sunglasses off her nose and shot Monroe a flirty look. 'You're too late. I plastered myself in cream before we came out.'

'And this would be relevant how, exactly?'

Seeing the mischievous twinkle in his eye, she giggled. The sound was light and girlish, just how she felt. 'Okay, you've persuaded me.'

Pulling the cream out of her bag, she threw it to him and turned over on the towel they'd arranged on the sand.

She could hear the rhythmic churn of the Atlantic behind them, but there was no other noise. Apart from the occasional jogger, the beach—reserved for use by the four houses on the promontory—was as good as deserted on a Sunday morning.

It was their last day alone together before Ali, Linc and Emmy returned from New York. As much as she wanted to see her family again, Jessie couldn't help feeling sad that the intimacy would soon be broken. The two weeks since she and Monroe had first made love had drifted past in a romantic haze.

They'd settled into a routine that had meant sunny, sexy afternoons and hot, insatiable nights. After their picnic at Montauk

Point they had got in the habit of going for motorcycle rides most days once she finished work at noon. Discovering parts of Long Island she had never seen before. They had romantic dinners by the pool most evenings. Sharing companionship and passion over seared tuna and white wine when she cooked and steak and beer when it was his turn. He touched her in ways she'd never been touched before, drove her to ecstasy and beyond. And every night she fell asleep, exhausted, content, her love swelling stronger in her chest with each passing day.

She adored watching him paint most of all, both proud and in awe of his talent. Had woken up only last Sunday to find him sketching her naked while she slept. She'd been horrified at first, but once he'd plied her with kisses, caresses and a shattering orgasm, she'd sat for him most of the afternoon and evening.

She'd asked him about his art. Why didn't he let Mrs Bennett take a look at the paintings? Didn't he know how good they were? Didn't he want to pursue his art as a career?

But he hadn't really answered any of her questions.

If she was being honest with herself, she had begun to feel a little uneasy about his unwillingness to talk about that or anything else more personal.

Ever since that first picnic he had been careful to keep everything light, relaxed. He hadn't asked her any more questions about her dreams, about her plans, her past or her future, and whenever she tried to ask him any about his own he brushed them off. Jessie had let him, scared to break the feeling of contentment, of unity, that cocooned them.

Propping her head on her hands, Jessie watched a lone woman stroll past in the distance, an energetic young puppy jumping at her heels.

Jessie closed her eyes, willed the doubts away. What was wrong with her? She was being silly. She and Monroe were in the first flush of their relationship and she should just lie back and enjoy it. All those big, serious questions could wait for another time.

The warm sun lotion sprayed onto her back and she stretched like a contented cat.

'Heck, this stuff's like house paint,' Monroe remarked from behind her.

'Factor fifty-five, otherwise I become one big freckle.'

His lips buzzed her shoulder blades. 'I like the freckles.' His hands began to massage the heavy cream in. She could feel the large, callused palms on her skin. She pictured his beautiful hands as she'd seen them late last night, stroking her into a frenzy. His hands, she decided, were the first thing that she'd fallen in love with.

Maybe she should tell him tonight how she felt? It was probably a record for her to have kept it a secret for this long. She'd already promised herself she wouldn't be hurt if he didn't tell her he loved her back, straight away. Didn't men always take longer to figure it out?

'You like that?' he said. She could hear the seductive smile in his words.

'I certainly do,' she murmured. 'Even though it's completely unnecessary.'

'Well, now,' he said, running his fingers under the strap of her bikini top. 'That's what you think.' Deftly, he unhooked the clasp.

'What do you think you're doing?' Turning sharply, Jessie grabbed her top and held it to her breasts.

His knowing grin turned devilish as his eyes flicked down to her bosom. 'I thought, seeing as you're European, you might find that unnecessary.'

'I'm not that European,' she replied tartly as she rehooked the bikini top. 'And neither are the families that live around here.'

He shrugged, keeping his eyes trained on her bikini top. 'You can't blame a guy for trying.'

'No, I suppose not.' She grinned back at him. 'Here.' She whipped the bottle of sun lotion off the sand, did a quick twirling movement with her finger. 'I think it's my turn.'

His lips quirked, before he turned over and stretched out on the towel. 'You know what? That was the other thing I was fantasising about,' he said wryly. 'Except in my dreams you were a lot more European.'

She laughed, pouring a generous dose of the heavy cream into her palms. She studied the lean, hard expanse of his back. The muscles had bunched up under his shoulder blades where he was resting his head on his arms. Spreading the liquid across the warm, tanned skin, she heard him give a low moan. She began to dig her fingers into the firm, smooth planes of sinew and muscle. He felt wonderful, she thought, and imagined what she was going to do with him that evening.

'You're too good at this.' He groaned. 'Don't forget this is a public beach, Red.'

She was having trouble doing just that, when the familiar ridges across his shoulder blades rippled beneath her fingertips. In the bright sunlight, the thin white scars stood out more prominently than ever.

'Did you get these in prison?' The question popped out before she'd thought about it. She regretted it instantly when his shoulders tensed. Her hands went still.

His past was one of the subjects they never talked about. From the little she knew about it, she guessed it was something he didn't want to be reminded of, so she had tried hard not to pry.

'No,' he said finally.

'I'm sorry, Monroe. I shouldn't have asked that.'

He rolled over, studied her.

She sat back on her haunches. What had she done? 'I really am sorry, Monroe. I didn't mean to bring back bad memories.'

Seeing the stricken look in her eyes, Monroe reached out, took her hand in his. 'Don't look so scared, Red. You're curious. You're entitled to ask.'

'I didn't mean to. It just sort of slipped out.'

She hadn't asked, he thought, although he knew she was curious. By not asking, she had given him her unconditional trust. And he hadn't done the same for her.

He'd told himself over and over that keeping things light, keeping things easy, was how it had to be—especially after their conversation at Montauk Point. He couldn't be her dream man, he didn't want to be, so there was no use pretending that they had anything more here than great sex and a good friendship.

But in the last two weeks he'd been more settled than he'd ever been in his life. He didn't know how it had happened, but gradually the restlessness that had been a part of him for so long had disappeared.

He'd fed off Jessie's compassion and her generosity, had

basked in her approval and had revelled in the passion they'd shared. But underneath it all had been the tug of guilt and the knowledge that, when it ended, leaving her was going to be harder than he could ever have imagined.

He could see, with the worry swirling in her eyes, that the reasons why he had deflected her questions weren't so clear-cut any more.

Had he kept silent because he didn't want her getting any wrong ideas about where this relationship was headed or because he was scared? Scared that once she knew all the sordid details of his life she wouldn't look at him with the same adoration, the same affection any more?

Should he stay silent, let the moment pass, or should he give her something back? Didn't he owe her that much?

He sat up slowly. 'I didn't get the scars in prison. My mother used a belt on us when we were kids.'

She blinked, stiffened. 'That's terrible.' The tear that spilled onto her cheek shocked him, and touched him in a way he would never have expected.

'Don't cry. It was a long time ago. It doesn't matter now.'

'Your own mother scarred you. Of course it matters.' She sniffed, wiping the moisture away with an impatient hand.

'She hated us. She had her reasons,' he said.

'What reasons could she possibly have for doing that to a child?'

The vehemence in her tone made him feel oddly comforted. 'Do you really want to know? It's ancient history.'

'Yes, I do.' Her eyes were fixed on his face. 'But only if you want to talk about it.'

Drawing a leg up, he rested an arm on his knee and studied the undulating sand and the insistent drift of the sea beyond.

Could he talk about it? Did he want to?

It was weird. He'd never felt compelled to talk about it before, but, oddly, with her he did.

He couldn't give her a future, he knew that, but would it be so terrible for him to give her a little of his past?

Jessie waited, watching his profile, her emotions a confusing mix of anger—at the boy he had been, the horrors he had suffered—

and anticipation. She so desperately wanted to know more about him. Was he finally going to talk to her about himself?

It seemed like an eternity, but eventually he turned back to her. 'The night before she had me arrested, my mother told me why she hated us. Me and Linc.'

'She had you arrested?' Jessie couldn't disguise the horror in her voice.

He shrugged, as if it weren't important. 'Yeah. Corruption of a minor, that's what I did time for in juvie. The girl was fifteen. I was just sixteen, so technically they were right. She was hot and she was as eager as me. I didn't stop to ask for ID.'

He picked up one of the small pebbles nestled by his feet, skimmed it absently across the sand. She noticed the ridged skin on his back and had to force the next question out.

'What happened when your mother found out?'

'One of her friends from the country club saw us together.' His shoulders hitched as he turned back to her. 'When I got home that night she was wired on the prescription drugs she popped like candy. She tried to go for me with the belt. Kept shouting at me, saying all this really ugly stuff. It didn't take much to wrestle the belt away from her. She told me then about what it had been like for her with my old man. How I was just the same.' He shook his head slowly, his breath coming out on a long sigh. 'First time I ever saw her cry.'

Jessie could hear the pity in his voice, but couldn't begin to share it, for a woman who had terrorised and despised her own children. 'What did she tell you?'

He looked at her, his eyes shadowed. 'That he'd raped her, repeatedly. That he'd wanted sons and even when she'd had several miscarriages, even after she'd begged him not to get her pregnant again, he'd forced himself on her. Forced her to have us.'

Jessie recoiled at the horror of it. What should have been a proclamation of love had become for Monroe's parents a proof of hate. Could it really be so?

'Did you believe her?'

He nodded. 'My old man was in his late fifties when she met him. She was seventeen, just off the plane from London, keen to find the American Dream. He was from one of Newport's richest families. She held out till she got his ring on her finger, then I guess she found out that it wasn't just sex he wanted.'

'What was your father like?' Jessie tried to keep her voice steady, not to let her disgust for the man who had sired him show.

He shrugged. 'I didn't know him. He died when I was still a kid. We didn't see him much. My mother sent us back to stay with our grandmother in Britain every summer.' He shrugged. 'When we had to be with her, we lived on his Rhode Island estate, but he had several other properties.' He looked up and gave her a hard look. 'He died of a heart attack. He was busy balling an eighteen-year-old showgirl in Vegas when it hit.'

He picked up a fistful of sand, watched it run through his fingers. 'He wasn't interested in us. Linc and I, we knew that, we were just a means to carry on the family name. But we never understood why our mother hated us. Her own mother, our granny, she was strict, but she wasn't twisted like her; she never once raised a hand to us like our mother did. After a while, I just kind of accepted it, but I know it screwed up Linc real bad. She beat on him the worst, because he would stand up to her.' He shook his head slowly. 'I guess the more he did that, the more it reminded her of the old man.'

'She hit Linc, too?'

'You don't know about that?'

'No. Linc and Ali have never spoken about his mother or father.'
He pondered that for a minute.

'Did you tell Linc,' she asked, 'what your mother told you?'

'No, he was long gone by then. He left when he was twelve and I was only ten. Our grandmother had died that summer. I guess he couldn't stand knowing we'd be stuck with her all the time.'

'You mean, until this summer, you hadn't seen Linc since you were children?'

He shrugged. 'Not since the day he ran off.'

Suddenly, so much became clear to Jessie. These men had been trying to forge a relationship after over twenty years apart, after the abject horror of their childhood, and she'd nearly messed it all up. 'I'm so sorry I behaved like such a silly cow when you arrived, Monroe.'

'Red.' He brushed a finger down her cheek, smiled. 'As far as

I'm concerned, you were feisty and gorgeous and you felt great wriggling around in my arms, so there's no need to apologise.'

The blush became more intense as she thought of their first meeting. 'Will you tell me about prison, Monroe?'

She wanted to know about the boy he had been—and how he had become the man she loved.

Monroe huffed out a breath. He had to do this. She had the right to know what he'd come from, how ugly it was.

'The first stretch was okay.' He couldn't even remember the green kid he'd been then. 'It was only six months in juvie.' He'd been wild and angry, he realised now, but determined to see it through and get out. 'I behaved myself, didn't attract too much attention. I was more bored than anything.'

The experience in juvie had made him think doing time wasn't so bad. It was three square meals a day and they didn't shout at you or beat you simply for existing.

'Ali said you did two terms?'

'Yeah, the second stretch was…' He paused. 'It was different.'

'How?' She said the words on a fragile whisper.

Monroe's gaze lifted to hers. Could he tell her? Would she despise him, for what had happened, for what he had let them do to him?

He took a slow breath. 'It was real time. After juvie I skipped parole, took to the streets. A year later, I was picked up in Buffalo after a bar fight. One of the local barflies went after me with a broken bottle. I defended myself and hit him back but then loads of others piled in. Glass and fists were flying everywhere. A guy got hurt bad that night. I wasn't from around there and I had a record, so it was me who ended up doing a stretch in the local pen. One of the meanest pens in the whole state of New York I found out after I'd been there less than a day.'

He could still remember the horror of that night, could still remember the fear afterwards, during two years of tests to make sure he was healthy. Looking at her, he could see the compassion, the understanding in her eyes. Maybe she wouldn't judge him, maybe she would understand.

'I had a pretty face. I was seventeen, cocky and stupid with it. I thought I knew the score.'

* * *

Jessie could see the shadow of bitterness in his eyes and felt her heart race in sympathy.

'They cornered me in the shower on the first night,' he continued, his voice low and thick with tension. 'Two of them. I fought back at the start, but what was the point? It was two against one and I didn't stand a chance.'

The tears slid down Jessie's cheeks. How had he survived?

He stared down at his feet in the sand. His words came out on a low murmur. 'They held me down, took turns.'

Leaning forward, she pressed herself against him, wrapped her arms around him and held on tight. She could feel the solid beat of his heart against her ear as she rested her head against the warm skin of his back. He didn't say anything, but slowly she felt his shoulders relax. He put his hand on top of hers.

After a long time, she let go, moved round, knelt in front of him. She gripped his face in her hands, made him look at her.

'You survived, Monroe. That's all that matters.' She could see the shadow of humiliation in his eyes, fought to control her anger at what he had been forced to endure, at what he was still enduring. 'Don't ever feel ashamed.'

'You don't think I'm less of a man?'

Where the hell had that question come from? he wondered. He'd never known the doubt was inside him until he'd asked her.

She flashed a seductive smile at him through the veil of tears. 'Monroe. I don't think I could cope with you if you were any more of a man.'

He brought his arms round her then, held her close, sank into the comfort and support she offered. He'd told her the worst of it and she hadn't been disgusted. She hadn't judged him as he had so often judged himself.

'Did it happen more than once?' she asked quietly.

'No, that was it. I got beat up a few more times after that, but mostly I kept to myself.' He folded his legs, settled her onto his lap, but kept his arms around her. And thought about how much he was going to miss her when he had to let her go.

* * *

As they walked back towards the garage apartment, the noon sun heating the grass beneath Jessie's feet, she considered what Monroe had told her of his past.

He'd been through so much, as a child and as an adult. Yet the only person he really seemed to blame was himself. She could feel the rough skin of his palm as he held her hand. He'd worked so hard, in dead-end jobs, yet he had such great talent as an artist but didn't want to promote it. Now she understood why—because he lacked the confidence.

She loved him. It wasn't just a silly girlish dream. It couldn't be. She understood him now. This was more than she'd ever felt for Toby.

She had planned to tell him how she felt tonight, but now she wasn't so sure. Maybe she shouldn't rush him, put pressure on him. He'd told her things she was sure he'd never told anyone else. He'd shared so much with her and that should be enough for now. She squeezed his hand as they mounted the apartment steps together.

'You all right?' he asked. The slight frown on his face made it clear he wasn't sure. The thought made her heart ache for him. How could such a strong, admirable man be so unsure of himself?

'Yes, I'm wonderful.' She glanced away. The heaviness of the conversation was making him uneasy. She needed to change the subject. 'It'll be nice to see Ali and Linc and Emmy again tomorrow, but I think we're going to miss the privacy.'

He pushed the apartment door open, held it as she went in ahead of him. 'I guess.'

'We may have a few awkward moments with Emmy when she comes skipping over in the morning to play mechanic with you.'

'About that…' He stopped dead beside her, the strain clear in his voice. 'We probably shouldn't say anything yet.'

'Why not?' Jessie felt the flutter of uneasiness in her stomach.

Monroe dumped their towels on the sofa. He took his time walking into the kitchenette and getting himself a glass of water.

'You want one?' He held the glass up.

Jessie shook her head. 'Why don't you want us to say anything to Linc and Ali?'

He put the glass down with a solid plop on the breakfast bar, looked at her for the first time since they'd entered the apartment.

'Is there something wrong, Monroe?'

When he didn't answer straight away, she felt a lump start to form in her throat. What exactly was going on?

'No.' Her relief at his words was tempered by the look of regret she could see in his eyes.

Reaching across the breakfast bar, he took her hand, pulled her around beside him. Putting his palms on her cheeks, he lifted her face to his.

'I can't let you go, Jessie. Not yet.'

She didn't know what to make of the statement. 'Why would you have to?'

He gave her a light kiss. 'Let's just keep it private for now, okay?' His voice was low, possessive. 'I want it to be just the two of us. I don't want to share you with anyone, Red. Not even Linc and Ali.'

'But, Monroe, how can we keep it a secret? If we're sleeping together?'

'Come over in the evenings, after they've gone to bed.'

She stepped back, a cold feeling in the pit of her stomach. 'That seems a bit sneaky.'

'It's not sneaky.' He snagged her hand, before she could take another step away. 'Listen, Jess.' He rubbed her palm absently with his thumb. 'Linc as good as told me to keep my hands off you.'

'Wha-at?' The shock came first. She pulled her hand out of his. 'I don't believe it. When?'

'The morning after the barbecue. I guess he could see I was interested. He was just protecting you.'

Shock was followed by indignation. 'But that's…' She spluttered to a halt, words failed her. 'But it's none of his business.'

'Sure it is. He's your brother-in-law.'

'Exactly, he's my brother-in-law, not my keeper. How dare he? I've got a good mind to give him a kick up the bum when he gets back.'

Monroe grinned at her indignation, making her more angry.

'What on earth are you smiling about? It's not funny.'

'Oh, yeah, it is.' He held onto her hand as she reeled away. 'I didn't tell you so I could see you kick my brother's butt.' He paused a moment, humour sparking in his eyes. 'Though that would be kinda fun.'

'Why did you tell me, then?'

He pulled her close, held her still when she struggled.

'Linc doesn't want me to touch you and I don't want him to know that I have.' He loosened his grip so she could see his face.

'But that's so Neanderthal of you both.'

His lips tilted. He didn't look remotely offended at the suggestion. 'I guess it's a guy thing. It's just… Linc and me are on shaky ground. I screwed up pretty bad with the birthday present.'

She sobered, remembering the painful incident at Emmy's party. 'Don't feel bad about that, Monroe. Linc understood. I'm sure he did.'

His hands stroked up her arms. 'He feels protective of you. I don't want to hit him with this…situation yet. Could we let it ride for now?'

She didn't want to let it ride. She wanted everyone to know how she felt about Monroe. That she was head over heels in love with him. But if she couldn't even bring herself to tell Monroe yet, how could she tell anyone else?

But still Jessie hesitated.

It was worse than sneaky not to tell everyone about their relationship. It was dishonest. But what could she do, seeing the insecurity in his eyes? He was worried about his relationship with his brother and, however misguided his suggestion might be, she couldn't stand in the way of him building a better bond with Linc. The two of them had been robbed of that in their childhood. She would not be the one to put a spanner in the works now.

'Okay, Monroe, I won't say anything, but just for a little while.'

Monroe pulled her into his arms, so she couldn't see the sadness in his eyes. 'Thanks, Red,' he said, knowing a little while was all they had.

CHAPTER FOURTEEN

'So, WHAT have you and Monroe been getting up to while we've been away?'

Jessie's fingers stopped dead on the garment she was busy folding into Ali's dresser drawer. 'Sorry, what did you say?' She could feel the heat creeping up her neck as she stared down at the newly washed T-shirt.

'Hmm,' Ali murmured from the soft leather armchair by the master bedroom's French doors. 'From the fantastic shade of red you're going, I'd say it's quite a lot.'

Jessie turned slowly to face her sister. She was trapped. That was the problem with having red hair and fair skin. She couldn't keep a secret from Ali if her life depended on it.

'Don't look so mortified, Jess. You've been here two weeks alone together and it was obvious the night of the barbecue there was an attraction there. I'm not all that shocked you guys went for it.'

Jessie stared at her sister, keeping her feelings a secret now seemed pointless. 'Actually, it's a little more than just sex.'

Ali studied her sister for a moment, then her eyes widened. 'My goodness.' She hauled herself out of the chair, waddled over to Jessie. 'You're in love with him.'

The depth of emotion in Ali's eyes made Jessie's own begin to water. 'Yes, I think I am.'

'How does Monroe feel?'

Jessie looked down as she closed the dresser drawer. 'We haven't talked about it.'

'Why not?'

'I don't want to pressure him.'

'But, Jess, you have a right to know how he feels, don't you?'

'He cares about me. I know he does.' He had made love to her so carefully, so tenderly the night before, it had to be true.

'What's the problem, then?' Concern tinged Ali's words. 'You don't look happy, Jess.'

'I…' Jessie paused, feeling guilty. She'd already broken the promise she'd made to Monroe. 'He didn't want you and Linc to know about us.'

'Why?'

It was such a simple question. Why did she find it so hard to answer? 'He says it's because Linc warned him off. Told him not to touch me.'

'That's ridiculous. Linc wouldn't say that.' Ali sounded so sure, Jessie's confusion increased.

'I know,' Jessie replied softly. 'After I thought about it for a while I came to the same conclusion. I mean, I know Linc can be a bit overprotective, but I'm sure Monroe got the wrong end of the stick somehow.'

'There's a very simple way to sort this out.' Ali headed for the bedroom door. 'We'll go and ask Linc what he said.'

'No.' Jessie caught up with her sister, held her arm. 'You can't ask him. I don't want Linc to know about this.'

Her sister stared back at her for a moment. 'I can't believe you and Monroe think you'll be able to keep it a secret. It took me about ten seconds to figure it out after we got back this morning.'

'Yes, well.' Jessie could feel the heat in her cheeks again but soldiered on. 'I don't think Linc's quite as astute as you are. He didn't spot a thing.' It had been almost comical, the way Monroe had been so careful not to touch her or look at her when the family's car had pulled up in the drive that morning.

'Linc was nervous,' Ali said. 'After what happened at Emmy's party. I told him to ring Monroe and talk to him while we were in New York. But he wouldn't do it. You know what men are like. They'd rather saw off their own tongues than talk about their feelings. But he's desperate to make things right with Monroe.'

'Monroe wants to sort it out as well, Ali.' Jessie pleaded with her sister. This she understood. 'That's why I don't think we should tell Linc about Monroe and me right now. They've got so much baggage to get through already. This will just cloud the whole thing. And anyway, we've only been an item for two weeks.'

'But you're in love with him, Jess.'

'I know, but it's still new. They've waited over twenty years to become brothers again. I don't want to make it more difficult.'

Ali plopped down on the bed, her eyes clouded. 'Did Monroe talk to you about their family, then?'

'Yes, he told me about their mother. What she did to them. What happened to him in prison. He's had such a tough life, Ali. He's had to overcome things I couldn't even imagine.'

Ali watched her for a long moment, then patted the bed beside her. 'Sit down, Jess.'

Jessie perched on the bed. She could see the worry and regret in Ali's face.

'All right, Jess,' she said. 'I won't tell Linc about you two.'

Jessie let out an unsteady breath.

'But I still think you're wrong about this.'

'Why? I—'

'I know you're doing it for all the right reasons,' Ali interrupted her. 'You're warm and you're giving and I think you've been waiting a long time to have someone to love.'

'Do you think I'm being a romantic fool?'

'No, I don't, Jess.' Ali's words were heartfelt. 'I don't think you're a fool at all. But,' she continued, 'Monroe is a very complicated man. He's not going to be an easy man to love.'

'I know that. But, Ali, he really needs me. And I think he's worth the effort.' How could she explain to her sister how special he was? 'He's such a wonderful person in so many ways. He's tender and caring and so careful with me. He's also fun and exciting and… Well, you already know how gorgeous he is. And, Ali, he has the most amazing talent. He paints, portraits, landscapes. In oil, mostly. But, Ali, he's got this incredible way of putting the emotion there on the canvas. I wish you could see his work. But he's sort of shy about it.' Jessie's heart felt as if it were going to beat right out of her chest. It was so wonderful to be able to talk to someone at last about how she felt.

Ali put her arms around Jessie, gave her a tight hug. 'I'm glad for you, Jessie. And Monroe. He's a lucky man, but I've got one word of warning.'

Jessie stilled her features, the concern in Ali's eyes stemming her euphoria. 'I'm listening.'

'By not telling Monroe how you feel about him. By not telling Linc about the two of you because Monroe has asked you not to. You're putting his needs above your own, Jess.'

'I know, but it feels right at the moment.'

'Fine, but it can't go on for ever. What you need is just as important as what he needs. Remember that.'

'Hey, you want a hand with that?'

Monroe looked up from the lawnmower to see his brother walking towards him across the freshly mown grass. He wiped his forearm across his brow as he stood up.

'All finished,' he said. 'I'm just gonna haul these clippings over to the garage. The garbage truck will get them tomorrow.'

Drawing level, Linc grabbed one of the sacks. 'Let me take one.'

Monroe bent to tie up the other. They walked in silence across the lawn with the cumbersome garbage bags in their arms. Monroe waited for his brother to speak. He could feel the sweat trickling down his back. It was a hot day; the mid-afternoon heat was a killer. He should have waited until evening to mow the lawn, but he'd been antsy ever since his brother and his family had got back from New York.

'Why didn't you come over for lunch? Ali was expecting you.' Linc's voice was neutral.

Monroe threw his bag into the large trash receptacle in the garage. 'Couldn't. Got caught up doing the lawn.'

Linc dumped his own bag into the bin. He slammed the lid down and then whipped around to face Monroe. 'That's bull.' He didn't sound neutral any more; he sounded good and pissed. 'Nobody asked you to do the damn lawn.'

Monroe's own temper spiked. 'I told you I'm not a damn free-loader—'

Linc held up a hand. 'Can it. I'm not arguing about that again.'

'I'm not the one who brought it up again.' Monroe bit the words out.

Linc dragged a hand through his hair, huffed out a breath. He didn't look angry any more, just miserable. 'Hell, Roe, why don't you come out and say it?'

'Say what?' Monroe felt a trickle of guilt.

'I screwed up. I know that,' Linc replied. 'I shouldn't have tried to give you the gift at Emmy's party. It was too soon. You weren't ready.'

'It's not that,' Monroe said, the trickle now a bitter torrent.

'You don't have to pretend with me, Roe. I know we don't know each other. But we were brothers once. I wanted you to remember. I was pushing you. I shouldn't have.'

Seeing the torment in his brother's face, hearing it in his voice, Monroe knew he couldn't hold out any longer.

'I do remember.' He watched Linc's eyes jerk to his, saw the rush of emotion in them. 'I remember you always gave me birthday cards. Some of the ugliest drawings I've ever seen in my life.'

Linc shrugged. 'I was never much of an artist.' His gaze was intent on Monroe's.

'I remember when I was ten.' Monroe's voice cracked a little, he cleared his throat. 'The last one you ever gave me. You said it was the Silver Surfer. Looked more like an icebox with wings.'

'Hey, I thought that was one of my best.'

'It meant something, Linc.'

Linc nodded, but didn't say anything.

Monroe swallowed, forced himself to continue. 'When you gave me that gift by the pool, it brought it all back. How it was when you were there, what it was like afterwards, when you weren't.'

Linc sighed. 'Hell, I didn't mean to bring all that back, Roe. I'm sorry.'

'Don't be an ass.' Monroe's words were sharp, angry. 'It's always there. So what? It doesn't mean a damn thing any more. You took me by surprise, that's all. The duffel bag's great, by the way. Just what I needed.' Seeing the pleasure in his brother's face, Monroe realised he should have said something much sooner. 'Thanks. It's the best birthday present I've ever had.'

Linc put his hand on Monroe's shoulder, squeezed and then let go. 'Not better than the Silver Surfer card, surely?' His voice was thick with emotion.

Monroe grinned. 'You got me there—maybe not quite that good. But pretty damn close.'

Ali's words of advice were still ringing in Jessie's ears when she tiptoed through the garden that evening. It was nearly midnight. The grass was cool under her bare feet as she skirted the Cape Myrtle trees, their branches bending under the weight of their summer blooms. She'd waited until the house was quiet before coming out. She could see the lights from Monroe's apartment blazing as always in the darkness, beckoning her back to him. The smell of lavender scented the sea air, making her smile with the romance of the moment.

She would tell him tonight. Ali was right. Monroe should know how she felt. Her love wasn't some burden that he would have to bear, after all. It was a joy, a gift. He could take it or refuse it or put it to one side and think about it. But whatever happened, she wanted him to know about it.

She remembered the difficulty he had had in accepting Linc's gift. The symbolism seemed so clear to her now. That was why she'd been afraid to tell him. Because she knew he wouldn't know how to respond, what to say. It seemed cowardly to her now. She felt so happy, so confident. He was the right man for her. He might be unsure of himself but he didn't have to be unsure of her.

She glanced up at his apartment window and saw his tall, lean figure standing next to the glass. He was watching her from the window. Her heart leapt into her throat. Her lover was waiting for her. She gave a quick, delighted wave, picked up the hem of her skirt and ran round the side of the building to join him.

As Monroe watched Jessie disappear from view, the weight of the guilt he'd been carrying around all day got heavier still. She had looked eager and so beautiful, the reddening twilight shining off that mass of fiery hair.

Bewitched, that was what he was. She'd cast some sorceress's spell over him. He was so desperate to hold her again, his hands fisted at his sides. It was getting harder and harder for him to contemplate letting her go.

When he'd bumped into her that afternoon and she had whispered that she was coming over tonight, he should have told her no, made some excuse. But he hadn't been able to. Not while he could smell that fresh scent of hers; not while she'd been looking at him with that combination of desire and trust that drove him insane.

So he'd told her to come, that he would be waiting. But as he heard her feet, light on the steps up to the apartment, as he turned and watched her step into the room, he knew that tonight he would have to start the process of drawing away from her. He would have to start putting the brakes on. He would have to let her see that there was no future for them.

'Monroe, don't look so forbidding. I'm positive nobody heard me.' Jessie ran across the room and clung onto his strong frame.

He hesitated for a moment, then his arms came round her, and he hugged her to him. She could feel the rough stubble against her forehead where he'd forgotten to shave again that morning. She could smell the wonderful musky scent of him that made her knees tremble.

'I missed you,' he said.

Jessie's heart stuttered at his words. Could he possibly have said anything more wonderful? 'Me, too.'

He pulled her dress off her shoulders, pushed her bra straps down.

'I can't wait. Is that okay?' That he should ask, the need and arousal thick in his voice, made her heartbeat skip again.

'That's good, because neither can I.' She laughed as he lifted her into his arms.

He carried her into the bedroom and in seconds they were both naked. There was little foreplay tonight, for none was needed. She was so giddy with the feel, the smell of him, that when he touched her core for the first time she was already slick and ready.

His tongue thrust inside her mouth as his fingers probed gently, stretching her and then retreating, stroking the swollen nub and making her cry out.

The heat was engulfing her, so suddenly, so shockingly. It was as if she couldn't breathe. She clawed the firm skin of his back as he pulled the condom onto his rampant sex. She gasped as he thrust inside her, filling her unbearably.

His hands tugged on her knees, forcing her legs wider still until he was buried deep. It felt like more, so much more this time.

The intense pleasure built to fever pitch as he moved in and out, the rhythm matched by her small, helpless cries. She was reaching now, trying to cling to the top; each vicious thrust seemed to take him further inside her, force her further over that edge. She cried out as she exploded over the top, shaking, shuddering, and dissolving into that wonderful oblivion. He sped up, thrusting hard, filling her to bursting. He gripped her hips, his eyes hot on hers, and she felt herself build again. So fast, so hard. The raw shock and arousal seemed to clog her throat, burn her to her core.

'Oh, no, not again,' she cried, on a pant of need and disbelief. The pleasure was so intense it was almost pain. He exploded inside her and shouted out as she shot over that last impossible crest and fell with him.

They lay panting together. Jessie watched the curtains billow beside the bed, the light breeze cooling her heated flesh. She was awed at how quickly the pleasure had overwhelmed her.

She propped herself up on his chest, looked down into his face and brushed the strands of hair back from his forehead. The satisfaction welled up inside her as she felt the moisture on his brow.

'I expect you already know this by now, Monroe. But I'm hopelessly in love with you.'

He tensed, but his eyes opened and fixed on hers. She didn't know what she'd expected to see, but the one thing she hadn't expected was regret. It was only there for a moment before his usual grin took over, but it was there for long enough to make the chill go right through her.

'You are, huh?' His voice was low, seductive.

'Yes, I am.' Now was not the time to back down, she decided. Maybe she'd been wrong. He didn't look regretful now. In fact, he looked cocky, his devilish grin dazzling her.

'That's sweet, Red.' His hands stroked up her back. Then he pulled her down on top of him, tucked her head beneath his chin.

She could hear the solid beat of his heart, feel the soft sprinkle of his chest hair beneath her cheek as the silence stretched out between them.

She wanted to know if he loved her, too. The question almost spilled out, but she stopped herself, biting down hard on her lip. The sea-scented air breezed through the open French doors, making her shiver.

'You cold?' he asked.

'No, I'm fine.' The words came out sounding stiff.

'Here.' He leant down and pulled the sheet up to cover them both. After tucking it around her, he settled her back into his arms, her head pillowed on his shoulder. 'That better?'

'Yes, thanks.'

Still she waited. Was he really going to say nothing more to her? She listened to the faint hum of the sea beyond the gardens. Could hear the murmur of his breathing. His arms were warm and strong around her. She could feel the gentle rise and fall of his chest beneath her cheek. Lifting her head, she looked up at the planes of his face in the shadows.

He was asleep.

Reaching, she caressed his cheek with one unsteady finger. She would not feel bad about this. She would not. Just because he hadn't declared his undying love, it didn't mean that he didn't love her. Her teeth tugged on her lip; her body trembled. She would not let the tears fall. She was not going to be a ninny.

She groped in the darkness for that feeling of euphoria, of contentment that had assailed her earlier in the afternoon when she had spoken to Ali. The glow of romance when she had looked up that night and seen him waiting for her. The exhilaration when they had been making love just a few minutes ago.

But the joy, the pleasure, refused to come. In its place was a feeling of uncertainty, of confusion, of rejection and, worse, that miserable feeling of foolishness she'd suffered so many times before in her life when she'd charged head first into something, letting all her defences down, only to discover that it hadn't been what she'd thought it had been after all.

CHAPTER FIFTEEN

'HELL!' Monroe shouted, shattering the quiet in the garage apartment.

The afternoon light was flooding through the French doors. The intoxicating scent of turpentine, sea salt and fresh grass swirled in the air.

It should have been the perfect time to paint, but he'd been trying to get this picture of Jessie on canvas for three hours and it wouldn't come. He'd never had this problem before.

Cursing under his breath, he dumped the useless paintbrush back into the mug of turpentine and braced his arms against the table top. He could feel the burning tension in his neck and shoulders. He'd hardly slept at all last night.

He picked up the washcloth, began to rub his hands, and then threw it down again, cursing more vehemently.

It was no good. He couldn't fool himself any longer. He should never have touched her. He could still see the confusion in her eyes when she'd told him she loved him the night before and he'd said nothing.

She hadn't asked him to say the words back to her, had let him hold her afterwards as if it were okay. But he knew he'd hurt her.

He'd pretended to be asleep, unable to face her, unsure what to say. And in the darkness he'd felt her tremble beside him. It had been like having a knife thrust into his chest, knowing she was crying over him.

She'd been so quiet this morning, seemed so fragile, he had forced himself not to touch her before she'd left.

He should have been glad. Maybe she had begun to see that what they had didn't stand a chance.

But he couldn't seem to get past what had happened last night. He wanted to make things right, even though he knew he couldn't.

And he missed her. Not being able to hold her this morning, not being able to bury himself inside her had put him on edge all day.

He pulled off his T-shirt and dumped it in the laundry basket he kept under the painting table. Picking up the washcloth again, he cleaned his hands and tried to ignore the grim thought that had haunted him since yesterday. If he was honest, it had haunted him ever since he'd first taken Jessie to bed.

What if he was falling in love with her, too?

He hung the washcloth over the table's edge, shook his head. What on earth was wrong with him? Of course, he wasn't in love with her. Any more than she really was with him. She was sweet and innocent and they'd both had the best sex of their lives together. That would dazzle anyone. But she couldn't love him; no one could.

He picked up one of the oils he'd been using, screwed on the cap. He slammed it into the box.

He couldn't let her go, not yet. The muscles in his back went rigid at the thought of it, with panic and more than a little pain.

There were still lots of things he needed to get done here, he tried to reason with himself. He couldn't be around her every day, see her every day and not want her, not want to take her to bed.

But there was one thing he could do, he thought grimly, and he needed to start now. He had to distance himself. So when he moved on, they would both be able to handle it.

He finished putting away the paints.

He needed to see her, to talk to her. He couldn't wait until tonight to get this settled. She should be back from the shopping trip with Linc and Emmy she'd mentioned that morning. He could stroll on over to the house. If he could just get her on her own for a moment.

He walked into the bathroom, stripped off his stained work jeans and stepped into the shower.

As the cold water hit him full in the face, he gasped. But once the water had heated up and he began to soap his tired, aching body, the tension inside him finally began to ease.

All he needed was to talk to her, maybe hold her a little, make love to her again. Everything could be as it was before. He couldn't tell her he loved her. Serious wasn't for them. But they could still enjoy each other for a little while longer.

Ali leaned back on her heels and felt every single muscle and sinew in her lower back scream in protest. She dropped the small garden fork clenched in her fist and tried to massage the pain away.

What had she been thinking trying to weed the flowerbeds while she was over eight months pregnant? She'd had some vague idea that it would help her forget the throbbing ache that had been pummeling her back all morning, but it hadn't helped a bit.

She was just trying to figure out how she was going to get up off her knees without a tow truck when Monroe strolled into view round the side of the house.

'Thank you, God,' she gasped.

Monroe spotted his sister-in-law immediately, her dress speckled with mud and her face contorted in pain. His heart skidded to a halt and then started beating in double time as he raced over and knelt beside her.

'Ali, what are you doing?'

'Digging my way to China. What does it look like?'

Okay, so she wasn't in the mood for kidding about. He took her arm and saw her wince as he eased her to her feet. Now he wasn't either.

'What was Linc thinking?' he ground out. 'Letting you loose on the garden when you're about to have his baby?'

'Oh, shut up,' Ali huffed. 'I put up with enough macho rubbish from him this morning before he left.'

'I see,' Monroe said carefully. 'So I guess the trip to China wasn't Linc's idea?'

Ali shot him a withering look, but her fingers tightened on his arm as she tried to straighten.

'Can you walk?' he asked.

'Of course, I can walk. I'm not an invalid.' The crankiness in her tone didn't dim the pain and frustration he could see in her eyes. It was starting to scare him.

'I don't know what makes men think that women lose all their faculties the minute they become pregnant,' she snapped.

The statement would have had more heat if she hadn't then groaned and clutched her back. 'Ow-w-w!'

'Forget this.' Monroe bent down and picked her up.

'Put me down. You'll do your back in. I weigh a ton.'

She certainly wasn't light. But he had no intention of putting her down as he marched across the pool terrace and into the house.

'Where's your bedroom?' he asked as he walked across the living room.

'You are not carrying me up the stairs. I can… Ah-h-h!'

He felt it then, the way her belly clutched hard and rigid against his forearm. She started to pant, tears sliding down her cheeks as she squeezed her eyes shut, gritted her teeth against the pain.

'Damn it, you're having a contraction!' His arms shook. She was in agony. What should he do?

The contraction seemed to last for an eternity before she opened her eyes and looked at him.

'Don't you dare drop me!' she said weakly.

'I won't drop you.' He'd cut his arm off first, he realised, before he'd cause this woman a moment of additional suffering.

He started up the stairs, carrying her as carefully as if she were made out of spun glass. But it made no difference. When they reached the landing another contraction seized her. She gripped his neck hard, the groan long and low, before she started to pant desperately again. He waited for it to pass before taking her into the first bedroom he came to. By his calculation, the pains were less than two minutes apart and lasting at least forty seconds. He had worked on a cattle ranch one murderous spring pulling calves so he knew it was not a good sign.

Neat and tidy and with no personal possessions in it, the room they entered looked like a guest room. He laid her on the bed, but she grabbed his arm as he straightened.

'Please, don't go.'

'I'm not going anywhere.' It surprised him to realise he didn't want to leave her. He gripped her hand as the next pain assailed her, rubbed her back until it passed.

He stroked her hair back from her brow. 'I'm going to go and get the phone to call Linc and the doctor. Okay?'

She nodded, meekly. 'There's a hands-free phone in our bedroom next door.'

He ran into the next room, grabbed the phone and ran straight back with it. He sat next to Ali on the bed and held onto her hand as he dialled Linc's cell phone.

'Linc, you need to get home. Your wife's about to have your kid.'

There was a crash on the other end of the line and then he heard Linc's voice. 'Is she okay? How is she?'

He could hear the panic in his brother's voice. Monroe fought to keep his own cool and even. 'She's doing fine.' He gave Ali a quick wink. 'She's a pro at this. But she wants you and Jessie here now. I'm calling the doctor as soon as I hang up, so just concentrate on getting your butt back here.'

Ali panted her way through another contraction as soon as he hung up.

'They're so strong, Monroe.' She gasped. 'I can't believe how strong they are.'

'I think we need to get the doc here,' he said as he began dialling the obstetrician's number that Ali reeled off, clearly knowing it by heart.

Reassured that the paramedics were on their way, he put the phone down. Ali was clutching the covers, her face set in grim lines of agony as she panted off another contraction. He gathered her into his arms and let her cling onto him. The helpless cries of pain she made until it subsided tore at his heart.

He eased back, looked into her face. 'How are you doing?'

She shook her head, tears trembling on her eyelids. 'I'm so scared. I've never done this before without pain relief. It hurts so much.'

He took her face gently in his hands. 'Ali, you're doing great. The medical crew will be here any minute, I promise. Just hold onto me and yell all you want. Okay?'

She nodded. He could see the pain swirl into her eyes again as her fingers dug into his arms. 'Here's another one,' she groaned.

She cried out in pain. Monroe heard a loud crash as the door slammed downstairs.

Monroe figured Linc must have flown up the stairs, because he burst through the door less than three seconds later.

'Ali, Ali, are you all right, honey?' Linc dashed across the room, his face whiter than the bed sheets. Ali shook her head, still panting, crying and holding onto Monroe.

As Jessie ran into the bedroom behind Linc she saw her sister cocooned in Monroe's arms. He held her gently as Ali's fingers fisted on his upper arms in a viselike grip and she screamed. At last, the cry of pain and anguish dimmed and Ali collapsed against him. He stroked her back, speaking softly into her ear. 'Linc's here, now, Ali. He's going to take over.'

She nodded weakly as Monroe pulled back carefully and stood up. He continued to hold Ali until Linc had taken his place on the bed.

'The paramedics arrived just after us,' Linc said softly to his wife as she huddled in his arms, exhausted. 'They're coming right up.'

Jessie blinked away the tears of emotion gathering in her eyes as Monroe walked across the shadowed room towards her.

He looked shattered, she thought. His eyes were swirling with an emotion so intense, so naked, it stunned her. She could see the vicious bruises already forming on the tanned skin of his arms where Ali's fingers had gripped.

'Where's Emmy?' he asked softly.

'We left her at Jill's house over the road, she's keeping her for the night.'

He nodded as he leaned past her to open the door.

She could hear the heavy tread of the paramedics coming up the stairs with their equipment.

'I'll see you later.' He glanced back briefly at Ali on the bed. 'You look after her,' he said.

He slipped out of the door, held it open as the medical team rushed into the room. And then he was gone.

CHAPTER SIXTEEN

HUGGING her newborn nephew in her arms, Jessie stared out the windows of Ali's bedroom at the garage apartment across the lawn.

Something was wrong with Monroe. But she had no idea what and no idea how to fix it.

It was almost three weeks since little Ethan Monroe Latimer's tumultuous birth, and Jessie felt as if she had been in the middle of an emotional hurricane. Being flung in hundreds of different confusing and conflicting directions. The wonder of her nephew's birth had been tempered by the fear that Monroe was drawing away from her and the rest of his family and she didn't know why.

The house had been a hive of activity since Ethan was born, but Jessie had welcomed the chaos. By concentrating on everything that had to be done, she'd managed to keep her worries about Monroe at the back of her mind. But she couldn't do that any longer. She had to face it. Something was very wrong.

'Is he asleep yet?'

Jessie turned at the sound of Ali's sleepy voice from the bed. She pulled the tiny bundle back from her shoulder and looked at his scrunched-up little face. 'Yes, he's out like a light.'

'You can put him in the Moses basket. He should sleep now for a good few hours.' Giving a huge yawn, Ali stretched and sat up.

Jessie kissed the soft fuzz on her nephew's head. She inhaled the sweet scent of baby before tucking him into the basket by the window. 'He's so gorgeous. I don't know how you can stop yourself from cuddling him constantly.'

As she said it Jessie caught sight of the garage apartment again through the window. The heavy feeling that had settled on her in the past few weeks came back full force. Monroe was never far from her mind.

'How are things going with Monroe?' Ali said softly.

Jessie looked at her sister. It seemed she hadn't lost her ability to read minds.

'We've hardly seen him since the birth, Jess,' Ali continued. 'Is something the matter?'

Jessie nodded slowly. Maybe talking about it would help. 'I think there may be.'

'Did you guys have a row?'

Jessie sighed. 'No, but in a way that's the problem. Something's wrong, but he won't talk about it.' She sat down on Ali's bed. 'It's really weird. But I think it has something to do with the baby?' And me, she thought, silently.

'How do you mean?'

Jessie frowned. 'I really don't know. But ever since the birth, Monroe's been—' She paused, trying to describe it. 'He's been sad, somehow, and withdrawn. And he's made all sorts of stupid excuses not to come over here. Not to see the baby.'

'I know. Linc's noticed it, too. He's pretty hurt about it, actually.' Ali shifted on the bed, the dismay plain on her face. 'Linc felt they were really starting to get somewhere as brothers. But now he says Monroe's shutting him out. And he's doing it with Emmy, too. She was crying yesterday because she said Monroe wouldn't let her help with the cars.'

Jessie bit her lip, feeling her throat close at Ali's words. 'I think he's going to leave, Al. It's like he's just waiting.' There, she'd finally said it. Her deepest fear. The thing she hadn't even been able to admit to herself. The dread flooded through her. She felt the first tear slide down her cheek.

'Oh, Jessie.' Ali reached over and wrapped her arms around her.

Snuffling loudly, Jessie pulled back, wiped the tears away impatiently. 'We still make love, every night. He's so tender, so careful with me, Al. But...' Jessie raised watery eyes to her sister '...I've told him I love him now, I don't know how many times. But he's never said it back, Ali. Not once. And every time I say it, I feel him pull away that little bit more.' She sniffed again, determined not to let any more tears fall. 'But I can't seem to stop myself.'

'It's nothing you've done.' Ali's voice was heavy. 'You've been honest with him. You've told him how you feel.'

'I think he needs me but he doesn't want to.'

Ali stroked her sister's hair. 'I doubt it's as simple as that, Jessie.'

'Maybe it's not, but, whatever the problem is, he refuses to talk about it.'

'Shall I tell you what I told Linc?'

Jessie straightened, nodded.

'I told him to give Monroe space.'

Jessie's brow creased. 'How do you mean?'

'Well, for starters, you should stop going over there every night.'

Jessie felt her heart sink. 'I've been an idiot, haven't I? He doesn't need me at all. It's just the sex.'

'No, that's not what I meant.' Ali grabbed Jessie's hand, holding her down when she tried to rise. 'I don't think that, Jess. He does need you. I think he needs you much more than he knows. But he has to admit it to himself, before he'll ever admit it to you. As long as you keep doing everything his way, he's not having to confront his own feelings.'

Jessie got up slowly, walked over to the bedroom window. She studied the garage apartment. He was in there now, she thought, painting. Waiting for her to come over tonight.

How hard would it be not to go to him, to deny herself what little joy they might have left? But what if Ali was right? What if, by not going, she could make him see what he was really pushing away?

She looked back at her sister. 'You're right. I know you are. But, Ali…' Jessie could feel the heat in her cheeks but forced herself to say it '…the sex is so wonderful. I never knew it could be like that before Monroe. I'm really going to miss it.'

'If he's anything like his brother, I know just what you mean.' Ali's eyes took on a wicked gleam. 'Linc and I haven't been able to do it for over a month. I'm ready to tear his clothes off now every time I see him.'

'Just listen to us.' Jessie smiled for what felt like the first time in weeks. 'We sound like a couple of nymphomaniacs.'

'Good sex happens to be essential to a happy life. Don't knock it.' Ali sobered, her voice going soft. 'But it sounds like you and Monroe already have that bit sorted. It's all the complicated stuff that needs figuring out now.'

'I still don't understand why you can't come over tonight.' Monroe struggled to keep the desperation out of his voice.

'I told you. I promised Linc and Ali I'd babysit so they can have a bit of privacy tonight. It's been weeks now since Ethan was born and they're…' Jessie paused '…they're ready to have a bit of alone time.'

Monroe's temper spiked. 'I get it. So because my brother wants to have his way with his wife, we have to do without.' He threw the paintbrush down that had been clenched in his fist.

'I'm sure we'll survive for one night.' Jessie didn't sound exactly devastated at the prospect, which bothered Monroe a lot more than he wanted to admit.

She turned to leave.

'Hold up.' He snagged her wrist, pulled her round. 'Where are you going now?'

'Out.' She hesitated. 'Just out.' He watched her teeth tug on her bottom lip. 'With Emmy. I'm taking Emmy down to the beach.'

He drew his hands up her arms. Stroked his thumbs across the sensitive skin inside her elbows. 'You sure you've got to go right away?'

'Yes. Yes, I have.'

He let his thumbs drift across her breasts, lightly circled the nipples. He felt her shivered response, saw her eyes flare with desire. He grinned. That was more like it. 'Can't you stay a little while?'

He reached up to caress her shoulders. Then slipped his fingers beneath the thin cotton straps holding up the vest-top she was wearing over a denim skirt. 'We could maybe, make up for tonight, before you go.'

He bent to nibble her neck. He knew she loved to be kissed there. Her head fell back, giving him better access. She gave a breathy moan and he hardened in his jeans. She smelt gorgeous, the light flowery scent she used making his nostrils flare as he reached down. He pulled up her skirt, slipped his hands under the lacy panties she wore. He massaged the soft skin of her butt with his fingers. He wanted her, now.

'Stop it.' Suddenly, she was pushing him away.

He watched astonished as she pulled her panties frantically back into place, smoothed her skirt down.

'I said, I've got to go.'

'What the hell's going on here?' He tried to snag her arm again but she raised her hand.

'Don't touch me, Monroe. We're not having a quick shag just because you're feeling hard done by.'

He scowled, the heat rising in his cheeks. 'What's this really about?'

She blinked at the shouted words. But then she skewered him with a look he could only describe as dangerous. 'You tell me. Monroe, what is this all about?'

He cocked an eyebrow, feeling angry and humiliated and more than a little desperate. Something had changed. Something important. He knew she'd wanted to make love as much as he had a moment ago. He knew her responses now almost as well as he knew his own. He knew how to make her want him, how to make her beg. It was the one thing he could give her. It had made her fall in love with him. But he'd persuaded himself over the last few weeks that, at least, he could give her something back. He could show her how he felt with his body even if he could never say it to her in words.

Why didn't she want it any more?

'I don't know what you're talking about,' he choked out. It was a feeble response, but it was all he had.

'You know what I think, Monroe?' She put her hands on her hips, her back ramrod straight and her eyes blazing. 'I think you're using sex as a substitute for communication.'

'What?'

'You heard me. Until you're willing to talk to me properly, I'm going to be too busy to have sex with you.'

She walked out of the bedroom. He caught up with her as she flung open the door to the apartment. Grabbing her arm, he hauled her round to face him.

'What is this—some kind of game?'

'No.' She yanked her arm free. 'It's not a game.'

'You want me as much as I want you, Red.' The bitterness, the desperation in his voice surprised him, but not as much as the anguish that flashed into her eyes.

'Yes, I want you.' Her voice broke on the words. 'You're absolutely right about that. But what I want a lot more is to know what the hell's going on in your head. And until you're willing to talk about it, the sex isn't enough. No matter how great it is.'

He stood there in shock. Horrified and dumbfounded as she turned and walked out of the apartment. She slammed the door behind her and he could hear her feet rattling down the stairs outside. But all he could do was stare at the polished oak of the door.

He wanted to stop her. To tell her he was falling in love, too, and it scared him to death. Because he could never give her what she dreamed of. He could never give her a happy family, stability, all the things that Linc and Ali had.

He walked slowly across the apartment. Standing at the window that looked out over the lawn, he watched her slender figure cross the grass. She was running, her shoes held in her hands, her hair fluttering in the light breeze. She was running away from him and he couldn't stop her. She wanted things, needed things he couldn't possibly give her. He closed the curtains, throwing the apartment into gloom as he shut out the light.

She'd been right; he'd been trying to hold her with sex.

He'd been devastated after the baby's birth. Had wanted to howl with frustration and anguish when Linc had told him that they were naming the child Ethan Monroe Latimer, after him. Because he couldn't have a relationship with this baby, any more than he could have a relationship with Emmy, or his brother, or Ali, or even Jessie. Not really. And the birth had finally made him realise it.

What if he gave up the rootless existence that had sustained him? The lifetime of roaming that now seemed so shallow and pointless? What if he stayed in touch with them all, became part of their family? He knew the answer only too well. He'd end up some bitter, lonely old man, watching their family from the outside, knowing he could never have what they had. Eventually the love he felt for them would be swallowed up by the envy.

So how had he consoled himself? By keeping Jessie close to him, by binding her to him every night, driving them both into sexual oblivion and hoping that it would halt her questions.

He'd started creating the distance he needed to create with Linc and little Emmy and Ali, but it had been too painful to do that and lose Jessie, too. So he'd used her again. Like some consolation prize.

He sat down heavily on the couch, stroked his hand slowly across the cushions where they first made love. So this was it, then. Either he had to tell her the truth or let her go.

He didn't have a choice. Not really. Not if he was going to survive with even a small piece of his pride—and his heart—intact.

CHAPTER SEVENTEEN

THE next week was torture for Jessie. Every night she had to steel herself not to creep out of bed and go to Monroe. He was like a drug and she a drug addict going through the worst kind of withdrawal symptoms.

Every night without fail the dreams would come. Powerfully erotic, devastatingly arousing. She would wake up covered in sweat, her nipples painfully erect, the throbbing in her sex so intense she could feel the heat flooding between her thighs. She'd actually taken to having cold showers in the middle of the night. Which made her feel ridiculous. And the lack of sleep had made her tired and irritable, added to which, for some odd reason, her breasts had become unbearably tender.

But worse than the exhaustion—and the knife-edge of unfulfilled passion—was the loneliness. She missed him, his teasing, his companionship, and his friendship.

She hadn't been back to the garage apartment since she'd issued her ultimatum and he hadn't come up to the house.

Each day Jessie became more convinced that Monroe would soon be gone. She checked the driveway each morning to see if the Harley was still there. Scared that he might leave during the night without a word to any of them. But, really, how much worse could it be? She felt as if she'd lost him already and it was almost more than she could bear.

A week after the whole nightmare had started, she was sitting by the pool with Ali. The baby was sleeping in the Moses basket in the shade beside their sun loungers. Linc had taken Emmy to the beach.

'Jess, you've been looking miserable all week. I take it Monroe's still being a complete baboon with you, too,' Ali said, leaning over the basket to check on the baby.

Jess shook her head, not sure she could talk about what was happening and not burst into tears. 'I haven't spoken to him since last Sunday.'

Ali looked up, shocked. 'But that's a week ago.'

'I know. Has he said anything to Linc—about his plans, I mean?'

'No. They're barely speaking to each other.' Ali sat back on her lounger. 'He was out yesterday morning pruning the privet hedge. I went over there to give him a piece of my mind about the whole situation. Linc's upset, Emmy's being completely horrible, as you know. Which is partly because of the new baby, I'm sure, but the situation with Monroe hasn't helped. I was pretty mad with him. I mean, he still hasn't come over to see Ethan yet. I was going to give him some serious grief about his behaviour towards the whole family.'

Jessie had seen him out there too, but had hidden in her room, clinging onto the small scrap of pride she had left. 'What did he say?'

Ali looked a little sheepish, then sighed. 'I couldn't bring myself to say anything in the end.'

'Why not?' Jessie was amazed. It was unlike Ali to back down from a confrontation, especially when the happiness of her family was at stake.

'He looks awful, Jess. If it's any consolation, I think he's suffering as much as the rest of us.'

'You do?' Maybe there was some small hope after all.

'I don't think he's been sleeping. He looks like he's lost weight. He was so tense I thought he was going to snap in two.'

Jessie could feel the rush of sympathy for him. Why was she torturing them both? She sat up, put her bare feet on the tile. 'Maybe I should go to him.'

Ali leant across, gripped her forearm. 'No, you shouldn't, Jess. He needs to work this out himself. He's like an angry bear licking his wounds right now. He's probably blaming you, me, Linc and everyone else for what he's going through. But once he figures it out, he'll come to you.'

'But what if he never figures it out, Ali? What if he just leaves?'

'That's a chance you'll have to take,' Ali said firmly. 'But I wouldn't give up hope yet.'

'Why not?'

'Well, for starters, while we were talking, his eyes kept straying up to your room.'

Jessie felt the bubble of hope swell inside her. 'Really?'

'Yes, really,' Ali replied, her voice rising with enthusiasm. 'And when I mentioned that Linc and I and the kids were heading back to London in ten days, he looked really worried. And then, you know what he asked me?'

Jessie shook her head, not quite as desolate as she had been.

'He asked me if you were going, too.'

Jessie woke up the next morning and for the first time in seven days didn't slip out the front door to check if Monroe's bike was still there. Maybe her dream wasn't completely dead after all. Maybe all this pain would actually be worth it. Maybe Monroe really did love her and he was going to tell her so soon.

It wasn't until after she'd shared breakfast with Linc and Emmy that something about the conversation the day before finally dawned on her.

The family was heading back to London in less than two weeks. She checked the wall calendar as she stacked the breakfast dishes into the dishwasher. Over the long lazy summer days, she'd completely lost track of the date. It was August twenty-seventh already.

Jessie finished clearing the kitchen and then rushed up to her bedroom and fished her diary out of the bedside table. She never could remember when her next period was due so she'd got in the habit of writing a small P next to the date each one started.

Flicking through the pages furiously, she got right back to July tenth before she found the little red P she was searching for. She stared at the date for a long time, then slowly counted the weeks forward. She'd made love to Monroe for the first time four days after that, on the night of Emmy's birthday party. And it was now the end of August. Jessie took a deep steadying breath, her heart pounding like a timpani drum in her chest. That was over six weeks ago.

She shook her head, tried to focus. This was ridiculous; she couldn't possibly be pregnant. They'd only done it that once without contraception. Monroe had been really careful to use a condom every time since; even in the throes of passion, he never forgot.

'Jess, I'm heading into town for some diapers. Is there anything you need?' Jessie's head shot up as she heard Linc's voice coming up the stairs.

'Wait a minute, Linc. I'll come with you.' Jessie shoved the diary back into the drawer and dashed to the closet, trying to ignore the flock of birds now swooping around in the pit of her stomach. She slipped on a pair of sandals, tied her hair back and began to plan how she was going to buy a pregnancy test at the chemist without Linc seeing her.

The stick was pink. A rich, lurid, candyfloss pink.

Jessie stared at the thin plastic strip in her hand. Dazed, her mind racing in a thousand different directions, she reached up and pulled the instruction leaflet off the top of the vanity. Had she read it wrong?

But she hadn't, and there was the proof in black and white—and pink.

She was pregnant.

Her fingers began to shake and she dropped the stick on the bathroom floor. It clattered, the noise deafening in the silence.

She was going to have Monroe's baby.

She looked down at her belly. Placing warm palms over it, she began to rock. What had they done? She loved him, desperately, passionately, unconditionally. And she loved this baby, too. The thought was so intense, so shocking, so sudden, that the tears started to flow down her cheeks.

But how would she tell him? What would he say? He wouldn't even talk to her about how he felt. He'd never even told her that he loved her. What if he didn't want children? What if the reason he hadn't come to see the baby was that he hated babies?

Jessie shook herself, pulled some tissues out of the dispenser on the vanity and blew her nose, wiped her eyes.

Don't be silly. He adored Emmy. He was great with kids. He

didn't hate babies or children. Something else was going on there, she was sure of it. But they'd only known each other for two months, had only been going out for six weeks and for over a week now they'd been avoiding each other. Maybe they had a chance of sorting the whole mess out, but bringing a baby into the equation was bound to make it so much more complicated.

As she sat on the toilet seat in the brightly lit bathroom, the worries just kept flooding through her mind.

What were Monroe's plans? She didn't have any real clue. What if her worst fears were true and he was planning even now to get on his bike and go? A single comment to Ali about whether Jessie was going to London or not next week hardly constituted a commitment on his part. She hadn't let herself think about what would happen if he did leave. What she would do. Until now. Now she had to. She hugged her belly again. And murmured a promise to her baby.

'We'll tell Daddy tomorrow. But whatever he says, whatever he does, Mummy will love you. Mummy wants you.'

'So let me get this straight. You're pregnant and I'm supposed to be the daddy?'

Jessie recoiled at the harshness in Monroe's voice. She had expected the shock she'd seen in his face a moment before. But she hadn't expected what had followed. He'd said nothing for what seemed like ages. Then his eyes had gone dark and bitter and he'd hurled the accusatory words at her.

'Yes.' Her voice trembled.

It had taken her all morning to pluck up the courage to come over to the apartment and talk to him. She'd wanted desperately to tell Ali, to ask her advice, but had decided that Monroe had the right to know first.

She hadn't slept all night, the questions hurtling around in her brain like dodgem cars, crashing against each other but never finding anywhere to settle.

Would he be angry? Would he be happy?

It scared her to realise she just didn't know. They'd certainly never talked about family or the future together. But of all the scenarios that had gone through her head while she'd toyed with her breakfast and waited for Linc and Ali and the kids to head off to the beach, nothing had prepared her for the coldness she saw in his eyes now. He looked like a stranger. Not the man she knew, not the man she loved.

'I don't think so,' he said.

'What do you mean?' Jessie felt her stomach pitch and roll. What was he saying?

'You really want me to spell it out?' The words dripped with contempt.

'Yes, I think I do.' Her voice broke, her throat began to close, but she kept her back ramrod straight. This had to be some kind of misunderstanding, didn't it? Where was the warm, caring, vulnerable man who'd held her with such care over the past weeks, had made love to her with such passion? Why was he looking at her like that?

'I'm not the damn father. I can't be. If you're pregnant, it's someone else's kid.'

The words were brutal and ugly, but it was how he felt. Monroe could see the tears starting to leak out of her eyes, the stunned horror in her face, but he didn't care. Monroe Latimer was too busy chasing his own demons.

He'd been through hell. He'd tried to leave, a dozen times. Had even got to the stage of packing his duffel bag. But then, he had to unpack it again. Like a damn lovesick fool. And it was all her fault. In his misery, he'd persuaded himself that she'd tricked him into this. He didn't do commitment and this was why. It caused too much damn pain. When she'd walked through the door, he'd been so overjoyed to see her, it had made him feel pathetic.

Then she'd made her announcement.

For a moment there, he'd wanted to believe it was true. It would have been the answer to all his dreams, all the things he'd wanted his whole life and never been able to have. But then the bitter truth had hit him.

It wasn't possible. It would have to be some kind of miracle. And Monroe Latimer was a man who didn't believe in miracles.

Either she was lying about the baby or she was lying about who the father was.

A longing, a yearning he'd thought he'd buried years ago had come slamming back to him. He could hate her for that alone.

The rage Monroe hadn't known still existed inside him rose up to choke him.

He wanted her gone now and he'd be as cruel as he had to be to get rid of her. The fact that the water flowing down her cheeks made him want to drag her into his arms only made him more mad. Even when she was conning him, lying to him, he still cared about her, he still wanted her. What kind of a fool did that make him?

'I don't know what you're saying, Monroe. But the baby's yours. I haven't…' Jessie could hardly say the words, to defend herself against a charge so cruel, so horrible. 'I haven't been with anyone else but you. You're the first person I've slept with in a long time.'

He laughed; the hollow sound hit her like a blow. 'You do that wounded look real well. You should be in Hollywood.'

'Please, Monroe.' She reached out, tried to touch his arm, but he flinched and pulled away. 'I'm not lying. Why would I lie?'

'You can plead and beg all you want. It won't change the facts.' He didn't sound angry any more, just indifferent.

'What facts?' The sob rose in her throat; her voice hitched as she tried to control it. 'Why won't you believe me?'

He dipped his head, shook it slowly, before looking back at her. 'I can't have kids. I had to give a sperm sample to the cops when I was sixteen. My sperm count's so low it's non-existent.'

Jessie felt the blood drain out of her face, grasped shaking hands over her mouth. 'But that's not possible.'

'It's possible all right.' He seemed immune to her distress, his voice calm, his eyes remote. 'You can see how it gives us a little problem with your announcement.'

She lowered the hands from her face, but she couldn't stop the tears, the tremors raking her body.

He really didn't believe her.

It wasn't a mistake, a misunderstanding. She could tell him now that he was wrong about himself. That somehow they had conceived a child. But even if she begged him to believe her, even if she had paternity tests when the baby was born, the truth would never take away the contempt he felt for her now. He didn't trust her. He didn't know she would never lie about something like this. So what exactly would she be begging for? The love of a man who didn't care about her, didn't know her or understand her?

The full horror of the situation finally dawned on Jessie. She wiped the tears from her face with the back of her sleeve. She put a hand on her belly, trying to protect the life growing inside her from the cold contempt of its father.

'I have to go.' She would have to get away from here, she knew, as far away as she could. 'I can't believe I was so wrong about you.'

'I guess I'm not as dumb as I look.'

It wasn't what she meant, but she didn't correct him. She didn't care what he thought of her any more. She couldn't let herself care.

She turned and walked away, her legs shaking, but her shoulders rigid. Once she had closed the apartment door, she ran down the stairs, her heart shattering inside her.

Monroe grabbed the coffee cup he had been drinking out of when Jessie arrived, and hurled it against the wall. He watched as the dark liquid dripped down the white paint.

He'd been fooling himself right from the start. He was madly, hopelessly in love with her. If not, why did her betrayal hurt so much now?

Jessie couldn't stop shaking as she stuffed clothes into a leather holdall. She had to get away before Ali and Linc got back with the children. She couldn't stand to see the pity in her sister's eyes, the fury in Linc's.

How could she have been so stupid?

She'd fallen in love with a man who didn't care about her at all. She'd foolishly thought that his tenderness, his care with her, the fun and laughter they had shared, the things he had told her about himself and his past had been the sign of deeper emotions.

It wasn't just her heart that had been broken, though. There was a life involved here. A new, unprotected life that she would be bringing into the world without a father.

As she picked up the phone to call a cab to the station Jessie dismissed the excuse that she hadn't chosen to get pregnant, that she hadn't planned this baby. She loved the life inside her, and she already felt totally responsible for it.

How would she explain to her child that its father didn't want it, didn't even believe it was his? That was the price her baby would pay for its mother's stupidity, its mother's naïve, romantic, ridiculously optimistic belief that she and Monroe had been meant for one another.

Going to Ali's bedroom, she located her sister's address book on the chest of drawers. She would have to talk to Ali soon, but she would not ask her for help with this. It felt as if her sister had spent all her life helping her deal with her mistakes. Well, maybe her affair with Monroe had been a mistake, but this baby wasn't a mistake and she was going to have to start making her life work for both of them.

She'd started something this summer at the Cranford Art Gallery. Mrs Bennett had told her only this week that she thought Jessie could have a career in the art world. In the haze of love and romance that she'd indulged in with Monroe she hadn't planned anything out, but now she would have to. She'd spoken to one of Ali's friends in New York last week who had mentioned a job in an art gallery in SoHo. Jessie had ignored it at the time, she hadn't thought she'd ever be moving to New York. Jessie took a deep breath. Her whole life had turned upside down in less than twenty-four hours.

She sobbed, quietly, unable to hold back the tears any longer as she jotted down Lizzie's address and telephone number. When she got to New York she'd contact her, see if the job was still available. Tearing off the page, she slipped the information in her bag then scribbled a note for Ali on the pad and left it on the dresser.

The loud beeping sound from the door buzzer made Jessie jump. Picking up her bag, she left the room and walked downstairs.

As the cab took off up Oceanside Drive, Jessie forced herself not to turn back and take one last look at the garage apartment. That wasn't where her future was any more. Despite the heavy weight of despair and humiliation, the sick feeling of fear, of devastation churning in her stomach, Jessie kept her eyes on the road ahead. She had a long way to go but she would get there in the end.

Monroe had destroyed her dreams, but he would never be able to crush her spirit.

CHAPTER EIGHTEEN

MONROE slashed the paint onto the canvas—the vivid red reflecting the violence bubbling inside him.

'Monroe, you in here?'

The shouted enquiry from the living room had Monroe dumping his brush in the turpentine. No doubt Jessie had gone running to Linc and Ali as soon as she'd left him. They would want him to go now, for sure. The fact that it hurt to know he would have to go only made him angrier. It took a titanic effort to plaster a cocky grin on his face as he walked into the apartment's living room and closed the bedroom door behind him.

'Yeah, what's happening?'

'I think you know what's happening.'

The sharp words and the heat in Linc's eyes made it clear he knew about Jessie. This was it, then, Monroe thought. The moment when his brother would cut him loose.

'I guess she went crying to you, then, did she?'

'If you're talking about Jessie—' Linc's voice was tight, brimming with annoyance '—no, she didn't. But she has run off to New York and, since you know why, you'd better tell me—and fast.'

Monroe shrugged. 'She says she's pregnant.'

Linc's brows shot up, before he exploded forward and grabbed Monroe's T-shirt. 'You got her pregnant? How the hell did that happen?'

He could see the fury in Linc's eyes, but it was nothing compared to the raw, bitter anger that was choking Monroe. Damn

Jessie for making him have to tell his brother something he'd never wanted to tell anyone.

'Let go of me,' he snarled. Pushing Linc's hands away, he struggled back a step, his own breath heaving. 'It happened in the usual way, I guess.'

'You son of a—' Linc jumped on him again and would have landed the punch but Monroe blocked the blow. They struggled for a moment, before Monroe managed to grab his brother in a headlock.

'Let me finish,' he snapped. 'If she is pregnant, I'm not the one responsible.'

Wrestling free, Linc turned and fisted his hands in Monroe's shirt again. 'How do you figure that?'

'I can't have kids.' The words came out on a broken shout as Monroe tried to shove his brother away. 'When I went to juvie I had to give a sperm sample. The police doctor told me my sperm count is practically zero. I only shoot blanks. Now do you get it?'

Monroe could see his brother had got the message, when his fists released.

Monroe looked away, unable to bear what he thought might be his brother's pity. He paced across the room, stared out of the glass doors. The tumbling waves in the distance matched his own churning thoughts.

'Hell.'

Hearing the anguish in his brother's tone, Monroe turned round. Linc had collapsed onto the sofa. When he lifted his face, Monroe realised it wasn't pity he saw there but concern and compassion.

'So when Jessie told you about the pregnancy, you told her it wasn't yours?' he said.

Monroe jerked his shoulders, tried not to picture her stricken face. 'Yeah, because it's not mine, it can't be.'

'Monroe, have you ever had yourself tested since—to make sure, I mean?'

Monroe felt his face flush at the quietly spoken question. 'No, why would I?'

'If Jessie says she's pregnant, she is. And if she says you're the father, you are. She wouldn't lie about that.'

Linc seemed so certain, Monroe almost wanted to believe it, but he couldn't let himself go there again. 'I'm not the father.'

'Monroe, you're going to get tested. I'll find someone near here that'll do it. If you won't do it for yourself, for Jessie, you'll damn well do it for me.'

'Why are you making me do this?'

Monroe could see the anger and regret in his brother's eyes, but his mouth was set in a firm line. 'You'll do it, Roe—you owe this family at least that much.'

As Monroe watched his brother walk out the door he felt temper take over.

How had he been suckered into this? The result was just going to humiliate him more. He thought of Jessie again and cursed. How could he have been so foolish as to break his golden rule? Never get involved. Never make a commitment. Now he'd made one, not only to a woman who could turn him inside out, but also to a family he'd never wanted any part of.

CHAPTER NINETEEN

'DR CARTER WILL see you now, Mr Latimer.'

Monroe threw down the glossy magazine he'd been pretending to read for the last half hour. Clinging onto the anger that had helped keep the pain at bay, he stalked into Carter's plush private office.

He didn't want to be here. He'd been forced into this and he was mad about it. He'd had to spend the afternoon yesterday giving sperm samples. If that wasn't bad enough, now he had to go through the humiliating charade of getting the results. He already knew what Carter was going to say. Had known it for most of his life.

The plump, grey-haired physician looked up from the papers he was busy shuffling and pointed to the comfy leather armchair across from his wide maplewood desk. 'Good afternoon, Mr Latimer. Take a seat.'

'No, thanks.' Monroe didn't want to sit down. He wanted this over with, so he could take the good doctor's results and shove them down his dear brother's throat.

'Well, Mr Latimer.' Carter put the papers down and studied Monroe. 'I'll cut straight to the chase. There's no point in beating about the bush, after all.'

Did the man talk in nothing but clichés? Monroe thought bitterly. 'You do that, Doc.'

'Simply put, Mr Latimer,' Carter replied, 'your sperm count is perfectly normal. In fact, I'd place it in the high end of the range.'

Monroe felt his heart stop. 'What did you say?'

'That you're not infertile—far from it, in fact.' Carter smiled.

Monroe dropped into the armchair. He felt as if his legs had just been yanked out from under him. 'But that's not possible. I was tested, when I was sixteen. The prison doctor said I was infertile.'

'Well,' Carter continued, 'that may possibly have been true at the specific time your sperm count was taken.'

'How?' Monroe's heart was banging away in his chest now as if it were about to explode.

Carter folded his arms on the desk in front of him and happily went into lecture mode. 'Mr Latimer, there has been a great deal of research into male fertility in the last ten to fifteen years.' Carter paused for breath, and then gave Monroe a self-satisfied smile. 'One of the most fascinating discoveries, in my opinion at least, has been how much the male sperm count can fluctuate given certain circumstances. All sorts of factors can affect the count at any one time. If you'd recently had a high fever, say, or were particularly stressed at the time the sample was given, it could wipe out the count completely or lower it substantially. But it would recover remarkably quickly. It's often the case that—'

'Hold on a damn minute.' Monroe's mind simply wouldn't engage. 'How the hell do you know that's the case with me?'

Carter sighed heavily. 'Mr Latimer, as I told you, your samples yesterday showed a high volume of active sperm. Whatever the test showed in the past, your sperm now are more than capable of getting a woman pregnant.'

Monroe staggered out of the office in a daze. Carter had droned on for another twenty minutes but he hadn't heard a word of it. His mind kept reeling back to Jessie and the anguish on her face when he'd last seen her.

There hadn't been any other guys. If he'd been honest with himself he'd known that all along. He'd had to work harder to get her into bed than any woman he'd ever met. And she hadn't exactly been the most experienced woman he'd ever slept with. It was one of the things about her he'd found irresistible—that captivating combination of innocence and passion.

Pushing open the double doors of the clinic, he walked onto the sunny street outside. But he didn't see the snazzy cars flashing past in the high-end neighbourhood, the afternoon shoppers rushing to make their latest purchase. All he could see was Jessie's shattered eyes, her tear-soaked cheeks.

A young woman with a toddler barged past him. Pushed to one side, Monroe leaned against the outside wall of the clinic. His legs were too weak for him to stand unaided. He scraped the hair back from his brow with a shaky hand.

She hadn't lied to him. She was having his baby.

Then another thought struck him and his knees gave way beneath him. His back scraped down the hot brickwork, until he was crouched down on his haunches. He stared blindly out at the legs of the people milling past on the sidewalk on a hot, humid Friday afternoon.

Jessie Connor had given him something he thought he'd never be able to have.

He was going to be a father.

As Monroe drove the Harley over the rise and gazed down on Linc and Ali's house by the sea, the tumultuous combination of euphoria, guilt and despair churning in his gut was making him feel nauseous.

How was he ever going to repair the damage he'd done? Jessie would hate him now; for all he knew she might even have run off to have an abortion. He sure as hell wouldn't blame her.

He shook his head, cruised the Harley down towards the house. He couldn't think about that. If she'd got rid of the baby, he would be devastated, but he would deal with it.

What was more important, what he wanted most, he realised with stunning clarity, was to get her back.

How would he ever persuade her that he loved her, that he had fallen head first before they'd even slept together, before they'd ever even conceived their baby? The whole time he'd been trying to keep his distance, his heart had been lost. Maybe that was the real reason he'd reacted the way he had when she'd told him about the pregnancy. Because he was scared to death, not just because he wanted it so desperately to be his baby, but also because he had always felt inadequate where she was concerned.

Well, he was going to have to get over his self-pity and all his self-doubts now. He was going to have to fight for her and he didn't kid himself it was going to be easy. But then he didn't deserve it to be easy.

Parking the Harley in the garage, he switched off the engine. First of all, he needed to find out where she was. He had to face Linc and Ali, tell them the truth and then beg them to help him find Jessie. What if they didn't want to help him? Why would they? After what he'd done to Ali's little sister, they probably hated him now, too.

'Roe, what happened at Carter's office? We expected you back over an hour ago.'

Monroe looked up to see his brother standing by the garage door. He pulled off his helmet, stared at Linc, unable to find the words.

Linc saved him the trouble. 'So Carter told you what the rest of us already knew. Am I right?' Pushing away from the door, Linc walked towards him. Monroe couldn't see the expression on his face with the afternoon sun shining behind him, but he didn't doubt that what he would see was contempt. Attaching the helmet to the bike's handlebars, he climbed off, ready to face it.

'The baby's mine.'

Linc considered the statement for a moment. 'Is that bad?'

'What do you mean?'

Linc crossed his arms over his chest and gave Monroe a steady stare. 'What I'm asking, Monroe, is do you want to be the father?'

'Yeah.' This part at least was easy. 'Yeah. I do.' Monroe jerked a shoulder, stared down at his hands, his voice thick with a yearning that he'd spent so many years trying to hide. 'Ever since I was sixteen, I never thought I'd have a family. I convinced myself I didn't want one. I always kept on the move, never made any attachments. I figured family wasn't for me. Seeing you with your kids, though, Linc, it made me so envious. Feeling Ali's baby kick inside her, watching her go into labour.' He sighed, dragged unsteady fingers through his hair. 'It hurt, knowing I could never have that.'

Linc took the few steps to his brother and pulled him into his arms. He held him close for only a moment, but that brief manly hug pulled them together through all the years of their childhood and adult lives when they had been forced apart. At last they were brothers.

Linc stood back, gave Monroe's shoulders one last quick squeeze. 'So, I guess congratulations are in order.'

Monroe gave a harsh laugh. 'Yeah, although I don't deserve any of them. I screwed up big time.'

Linc nodded. 'I can't argue with you there, Roe. Question is, what do you intend to do about it?'

'I want her back, Linc. Not just because of the baby.' Monroe ground his fists down into the pocket of his jeans. 'I'm not kidding myself. After the way I treated her, there may not even be a baby any more.'

'Don't sell her short again, or I'll have to get mad at you.' Linc put a hand on Monroe's shoulder. 'You realise you're going to have to do some serious explaining and probably more than your fair share of grovelling if you're going to fix this?'

Monroe didn't like the sound of that 'if' but said nothing.

'It's up to you now to get Jessie and your baby back, Roe.'

Monroe shrugged Linc's hand off. 'Do you think I don't want that?' He raked shaking fingers through his hair, despair settling on him like a lead weight. 'But I don't even know where to start. I don't even know where she is.'

'Ali does.'

Monroe's head jerked up.

'Jessie phoned last night to make sure we weren't worried about her.'

'Where is she?'

'I don't know. Jessie asked Ali not to tell me. I guess she figured I might tell you.'

Monroe's shoulders slumped. 'How am I gonna find out, then?'

'You'll have to ask Ali.'

'Are you kidding me? She won't tell me. It's a miracle you don't hate me, but she must after what I did to her sister.'

'Monroe.' Linc huffed out a breath. 'You are one stupid guy sometimes.' He gave Monroe a wry smile. 'Ali doesn't hate you. She wants to see you and Jessie work this out as much as I do.'

'Really?' Monroe felt the first stirrings of hope since he'd stumbled out of Dr Carter's office that afternoon. Maybe there was a small chance he might be able to pull this off.

'Where is she, Ali?'

'Monroe, Jessie told me in confidence,' Ali said softly, cradling her sleeping son in her arms. 'She didn't specifically tell me not to tell you, but I think that's only because she didn't think you'd care.'

'Damn it.' The baby flinched, making Monroe soften his voice. 'Sorry.' He touched the baby's head, and his heart stuttered at the soft, warm feeling before he stuffed his hand back in his pocket. 'I have to talk to her, Ali. I have to at least try.'

'I understand that.' Reaching up, Ali touched his arm. 'Sit down, Monroe.'

He plopped down on the sofa opposite her, his body rigid with tension.

'Is it just because of the baby that you want to contact Jessie?'

'No.' The denial came so quickly, so forcefully, he knew it was the truth. He paused, though, and stared at the hands clenched in his lap. 'No, it's not just because of the baby.'

How could he make Ali understand what he had done, if he didn't really understand himself?

'I love her, Ali. I think I knew that even before Carter told me the truth. I was just too scared to admit it. I've always known I didn't deserve her.'

He stood up, walked over to the window and stared out at the pool. The sight reminded him of the first time they'd met.

'Why do you think you don't deserve her?' Ali asked quietly from behind him.

The note of incredulity in her voice made Monroe shake his head as he turned back to her. 'Because I'm an ex-con. I've got no money and not a lot of prospects. The only thing I own is a Harley and the clothes on my back. And even if that meant nothing, even if we could get past all of that, I didn't think I would ever be able to offer her kids. I knew how much she wanted them. How much she wanted a family. She told me that was her dream.'

Ali sighed, adjusting the baby in her arms. 'You know what I think?'

He almost smiled, the clipped, precise note of irritation in her voice reminding him of Jessie.

'I think you're an idiot.'

'Thanks.' He did smile then, realising that he hadn't just found a brother in the last few months, he'd also found a sister.

Getting up, Ali tucked the baby carefully into its crib before walking back to Monroe. The look she gave him was more annoyed than sisterly, though.

'Firstly, you were little more than a child when you went to prison. Secondly, we know now that the baby-making thing isn't going to be a problem.' The look she gave him was direct enough to make his face heat. 'As for the no money and no prospects, we both know that's a load of rubbish, too.'

'How do you figure that?' Monroe raised his voice in exasperation. This was not the reaction he had expected.

'Jessie told me about your artwork.' He felt the flush deepen on his face as she continued. 'Jessie knows art, she's studied it and she's convinced you could have a career as an artist. So I think if you're worried about money and prospects, Linc has a friend called Carole Jackson who owns a very successful gallery in New York—you should contact her and let her take a look at the stuff you've been working on for the last two months.'

Monroe straightened. 'I'm not asking favours from one of Linc's friends.'

'Oh, don't get your knickers in a twist.' Ali waved her hand impatiently. 'I know how important pride is to you. But it's misplaced here. Carole's a tough lady and she has one of the best and most influential independent galleries in New York. She's not going to agree to exhibit anything unless she thinks it's outstanding. The question here is, do you have the guts to try? Or are you going to spend the rest of your life hiding behind your insecurities?'

Annoyed and embarrassed at one and the same time, Monroe had to force himself not to pout. 'We're getting off the point here. I want to know where Jessie is. I didn't come here to get a lecture about my insecurities.'

'Well, tough, you happen to need one.' Ali's face lit up, as if she had been struck by divine inspiration. Then her eyes narrowed and she gave Monroe a look that he could only describe as sneaky. 'I tell you what, Monroe. These are my terms. You call Carole and get her to have a look at your work. Whatever she says, once she's seen it I'll let you know where Jessie is.'

Monroe blinked in astonishment. 'You're not serious?'

'Yes, I am,' came the sharp, no-nonsense retort. 'And another thing.'

'I don't want to hear this,' he muttered.

'Well, that's a shame, because you're going to. I think it's about time you started making something of your life, Monroe. You were forced to cope with some terrible things in your childhood and your adolescence. But I think you've spent enough time running away from them, don't you?'

He didn't bother to answer the rhetorical question, just fumed in stony silence.

'You're thirty-two years old.' Ali's voice was firm. 'And in about seven and a half months' time you're going to be a father to boot. When you see Jessie again, you'll need to offer her a bit more than a grovelling apology and a declaration of undying love.'

'Who said I was going to grovel?' His angry words were answered with a disdainful look.

'You'll need to show Jessie that you've changed. That you've got something to offer her and the baby. That you're running towards something now.'

'But what if this woman hates my stuff?' He snarled the words, but even he could hear the insecurity behind them.

'Do you think your work is any good, Monroe?'

He shrugged. 'I mostly get what I aim for.'

'Then that's all the answer you need, isn't it?'

Monroe was furious. He'd been cornered, but he could see from the determination in Ali's face that he wasn't going to be able to charm or bluff his way out of this one.

'Hell, okay, I'll call this Carole Jackson today. But whatever she says you'll tell me where Jessie is, right?'

'Of course I will. A deal's a deal.'

After watching her brother-in-law stalk out of the room, Ali walked over to the crib. Leaning down, she stroked an unsteady hand down her newborn son's downy cheek.

'I hope your auntie doesn't kill me for this, when your uncle turns up on her doorstep.'

CHAPTER TWENTY

JESSIE stepped out of the glass-fronted art gallery onto the bustling Prince Street sidewalk. She'd done it. She'd got the job. She should be overjoyed.

The assistant sales position was low-paying but Cullen's was a well-respected Manhattan gallery and the job had prospects with a capital P.

This was the sort of opportunity she wouldn't even have dreamt of when she'd left London to join Ali and her family in the Hamptons.

She ducked into the tiny coffee shop to get out of the sweltering hustle and bustle of lunchtime SoHo, ordered a herbal tea at the counter and then sat down at the only available booth. She needed to get in touch with Ali, who had been leaving messages demanding that she call her for the last few days. But she dumped her bag on the table and left the phone inside. Staring blankly out at the busy street through the café window, she absently rested her hand on her still-flat belly. She took the peppermint teabag out of the earthenware mug and sipped the steamy brew.

The joy wouldn't come.

Had Monroe destroyed this for her, too?

She couldn't stop the anger, the resentment and misery from welling up inside her. With this new job, she was beginning the brilliant career she had always dreamed of. But after what had happened with Monroe, she wondered how long it would be before she'd find joy in anything again.

She finished the last of the tea, grateful that the usual nausea didn't come. Her hand rested again on her stomach and she glanced down.

When would she feel the baby kick for the first time?

The errant thought made her smile. Maybe it wouldn't be so long before she felt joy again after all. Despite the horror of what had happened with the baby's father, every time she thought about the baby her pulse jumped with excitement and anticipation.

She sighed. As usual she was getting ahead of herself. At the moment, the only sign of her pregnancy was incredibly tender breasts and the fact that for the last few days she'd been hideously sick every morning.

She blinked furiously as her eyes began to glaze over again. Grabbing her bag, she pulled out her tissues. It must be the pregnancy hormones. Her emotions were all over the place. Yes, she was ecstatic about the baby, but she was also dreading having to deal with its father.

Ali had called her two days ago to tell her Monroe had been tested and now knew the truth. He was the father.

Jessie blew her nose and stuffed her tissues back in her bag. All right, sooner or later she'd have to deal with him. As much as she hated to admit it, she knew he would want to have a part in the baby's life.

But that didn't mean he had to have a part in hers, she thought bitterly. She wasn't the romantic fool she'd been just a week ago— blinded by her optimism, her immaturity and her love from seeing him for what he really was. A hard man who'd been forced to make hard choices in his life. A man who would never trust and appreciate her, had probably never really trusted or appreciated anybody. Over the last few days, she had accepted the fact that a part of her heart would always be lost to him, but she couldn't risk her happiness— or her child's happiness—on a man who could never love her back.

Here she was thinking about him again when she should be out celebrating her new job, the new life she was about to embark on.

Reaching into her bag, Jessie pulled out her cell phone and started keying in a text message to Ali. Her eyes jerked up when someone slid into the booth opposite.

'Hello, Red.'

The phone slid out of her hand and thudded onto the Formica table.

* * *

Monroe had been following Jessie since she left Cullen's.

He'd caught the first train out of the Hamptons that morning, as soon as he'd gotten the call from Carole Jackson. He still couldn't quite believe the lady was planning a major debut show of his work in her ritzy uptown gallery.

He had checked into the room Jackson had booked him at the Waldorf that morning, feeling like a vagrant in his ragged denims and faded T-shirt. He'd put off the meeting with Carole and her staff until tomorrow, though. He had more important business to conduct in New York and it couldn't wait any longer.

He'd tracked down Jessie's whereabouts and raced down to SoHo, the nerves over what lay ahead nearly making him miss his stop on the subway.

He'd spotted Jessie leaving Cullen's. Seeing her again had made his heart pound like a jackhammer. But he hadn't had the guts to go up to her on the street. When she'd walked into the nearby coffee shop, it had seemed perfect. He could confront her there. But when she'd slipped into the booth, still he'd held back. Even after seven long days of going over everything in his head, he didn't know what the hell to say to her to make it right. The creeping feeling in the back of his mind, that she might have had an abortion, wouldn't go away. He couldn't let that cloud things, but it did. He'd hate himself even more if she had, because that would be his fault, too.

He tried to plaster a smile on his face. Look easy, don't look desperate, was the only thing that kept going through his head as he sat down opposite her.

'You look great, Red.'

The ice in Jessie's chest turned to fire.

'You bastard.' Grabbing her phone, she turned. She had to get out of here.

He leant over and took her arm.

'Let go of me,' she snarled, trying to yank her arm free.

He didn't let go, but got up and slid onto the seat beside her. 'Calm down, Red.'

She glared at him. Boxed in. 'Don't you tell me to calm down, you…you…' she couldn't think of a word bad enough '…you bastard.'

'All right, fine. Letting go.' Monroe lifted his hands, looking defeated.

'Get out of my way.' She tried to push past him.

He didn't budge. 'Jess, we need to talk.'

'We do not need to talk,' she snapped. 'There is absolutely nothing I want to say to you.'

'I figured that,' he said as he ploughed his fingers through his hair. 'But there's something I've gotta say to you.'

She tried to push past him again. He held firm.

'I'm sorry, Red,' he said, touching her arm. 'You don't know how sorry I am for what I said. About you, and about the baby.'

She felt herself weaken. Just for a moment. She could hear the torment in his voice, see the misery in his eyes. She could imagine how much he had suffered all those years, thinking he couldn't have a child. But then he reached up and ran his finger down her cheek. She jerked her head away, the gesture bringing back a rush of memories.

'Don't touch me.' She slapped his hand away. 'I don't want to hear that you're sorry,' she cried. 'I don't care that you're sorry.' A thought struck her and she felt as if she might break apart. 'You're only sorry now because you found out the baby's yours.'

He flinched.

'I'm right, aren't I?' she said. 'That's the reason you're here?'

'It's not the only reason.' He paused, seemed to think about it for a moment. 'But it is one of them.'

'I knew it.' Jessie's voice shook on the words.

'Is there still a baby, Jessie?'

Jessie could hear the anguish in his voice, see the fear in his eyes and the urge to hurt him as badly as he had hurt her over-whelmed her.

'No, there isn't.' The lie lay like lead on her tongue the minute she'd said it.

He cursed, closed his eyes and let his head fall back onto the high leatherette seat of the booth.

I don't care, Jessie told herself silently. I don't care if I've hurt him.

But then he turned and studied her. Instead of the bitterness, the anger she had expected, there was just a terrible sadness in his gaze. 'Jess. I'm sorry for that, too, then,' he said softly.

She would have told him the truth then, would have done anything to take the self-loathing out of his eyes, but the wave of nausea hit without warning.

'Oh, get out of my way.'

'What is it?' he said, lifting his head off the seat.

'Mo-o-ove!'

He jumped back. Jessie rushed past him, her hands clasped over her mouth.

She managed to make it to the kerb outside before her stomach heaved.

When the vomiting finally stopped, her legs started to wobble. She was about to collapse in a heap when strong arms wrapped around her waist and held her upright.

'I've got you, Red.'

He handed her some napkins. The shrill whistle in her ear made her jerk. A yellow cab screeched to a stop in front of her and she was lifted against his chest.

'What are you doing?' she said weakly. 'Leave me alone.'

'Not a chance.'

Monroe settled her on the cab seat before giving the driver quick instructions. Jessie wanted to rise, to get away, but her legs simply wouldn't do what she told them. He lifted her effortlessly into his lap as the car sped off into the midday traffic.

'I can sit on my own, thanks.'

She struggled, but he held her in place.

His lips curved slightly. 'Forget it, Red. We're going to have that talk.'

She stared at him in astonishment. 'What the heck are you smiling about?'

'So there's not still a baby, huh?' The light dancing in his deep blue eyes made it clear it was a rhetorical question.

'Well…' She'd made a fool of herself.

Okay, so she was glad he didn't look stricken any more. But he didn't have to look quite so ecstatic. That was just plain annoying.

'All right, there is still a baby. I lied.' She sounded huffy. She didn't care. 'I said that because I wanted you to suffer.'

Despite the catty remark, he grinned. 'Yeah, I figured that out while I was watching you decorate the sidewalk.'

Parting the jacket of her linen trouser suit, he stroked his palms over her midriff, stared down at it. She could see the fierce pride and joy in his face, struggled hard not to be moved by it.

'How big is he in there—d'you know?' he said.

'Who says it's a he?'

'You think it's a girl?' It was as if he hadn't heard the sneer in her words. 'That'd be so cool.' His gaze stayed on her belly; his hands felt warm through the thin fabric of the pink silk camisole.

Without saying anything, she pushed his hands away and wriggled off his lap. He didn't stop her as she shifted as far away from him as she could get. Turning her back to him, she stared out of the cab window.

She didn't want to see the joy in his face, didn't want to see his intense happiness at the baby. It might make her forget what he was really like. It might make her forget what he'd put her through.

Monroe let her go, his euphoria fading. Yeah, there was still a baby, the best gift anyone had ever given him, could ever give him. But he wanted so much more. He wanted Jessie, too. And the problems between them were far from solved.

'Jess, I can say I'm sorry for the rest of my life. But it won't ever undo what I said. It can't ever take away the wrong I did you. I know that.'

When she turned, he saw the sheen of tears in her eyes and felt his heart clutch at the sight.

'Just tell me one thing,' she whispered. 'Did you really think I'd slept with someone else?'

He shook his head. 'No.' About that he could be honest. 'Not when I thought it through. I just…' He stopped. How could he make her understand? 'I never thought I could have kids, Jess. I'd spent my whole life convincing myself I didn't want them. When you told me, I wanted so bad for it to be true.'

'Why didn't you believe me, then?'

What did he say to that?

The cab came to a stop and the driver opened his grill. 'We're here, buddy.' Monroe slapped a twenty into his palm and guided Jessie out.

'Why have you brought me here?' Jessie said, gaping at the ornate art-deco frontage on the landmark hotel.

'I'm staying here.'

'You are?' She looked stunned.

He shrugged. 'Yeah, the gallery's paying for it.'

'What gallery?'

He didn't want to go into all that now. This was more important.

'It's a long story.' He took her elbow, guided her towards the stairs. 'I've got a suite. I can order in room service. If you want, you know. If you're hungry now. We can talk.'

She pulled back, looking confused and wary. 'You don't have to explain anything to me, Monroe. Not really.'

Monroe didn't like that look of resignation, or the note of finality in her voice.

'Yeah, I do.' Of that he was certain, but how to do it was a whole other question.

She clutched her hands together, stared down at them. 'I won't keep the baby from you,' she said, and looked up. 'You can still be a part of its life. I wouldn't keep your child from you. I know how much it means to you.'

He let her run down before he spoke.

'Hell, Red. I know that. But the baby's not what this is about.'

'Of course it is, Monroe,' she said reasonably. 'But the point is, now you know you can have kids, this won't be the only baby. You can have other kids, they don't have to be with me.'

Looking at her on the steps of the Waldorf, wringing her hands and trying to be fair to a man that had as good as flayed her alive, Monroe knew he would never want anything again the way he wanted her.

'We can talk about visitation rights once the baby's born,' she continued in a murmur, 'but until then, I don't want to—'

'Jessie, stop being so damn noble for a minute and let me say what I need to say.'

Okay, so that wasn't exactly diplomatic, he thought as he saw her stiffen. But he was feeling raw at the prospect of what he was going to have to do next. Grovelling, he realised, didn't even come close.

'Don't you dare shout at me,' she shouted back at him.

He wanted to grab her and carry her into the hotel, but figured that wasn't going to work either. 'Jess,' he sighed. 'Will you please just come upstairs?'

She stared at him for what seemed like forever. When she spoke her voice was quiet, her eyes wary. 'I'll come on one condition.'

'Sure. What is it?'

'You promise not to touch me.'

He felt the sharp stab of pain and regret, but nodded.

Silence suited her fine, Jessie thought as Monroe picked up his key card at the reception desk and directed her to one of the dark-panelled lifts in the foyer. He was careful not to put his hand on the small of her back as he had always done before, she noticed, and was grateful. Seeing him again had been enough of a jolt to her system without him touching her. The fact that her hormones had responded as they always did to his hard, leanly muscled frame and that magnificent face just made her feel twice as vulnerable.

Why did he have to look so flipping gorgeous?

She tried hard to recall the cruel things he had said to her, the sneer on his face when he'd told her the baby wasn't his, but as the lift glided smoothly up to his floor she could see no trace of it on his face. He looked tense and nervous, tapping the key card against his thigh as he studied the elevator's indicator lights. He hadn't so much as glanced at her since she'd agreed to come to his room. That cool, confident charm that had always been a part of him was gone.

He led her down to the end of the wide hallway and slipped the key card into ornately carved double doors with a panel on them that read 'The Ambassador Suite.'

Jessie gaped as she stepped into a huge, lushly carpeted sitting area ahead of him. Three long mullioned windows across the room showcased the New York skyline in all its glory.

Monroe dumped the card on a small table next to one of the two large leather sofas that dominated the room. 'Have a seat.' He gestured to the sofa. 'You want a drink?'

'Water's fine.' She sat down stiffly and tried to quell her curiosity. Where had he got the money for this place, and what was that he'd said about a gallery?

None of your business, she thought ruthlessly as he turned from the minibar with a pricey bottle of Scottish mineral water and a glass in his hand.

Passing the drink to her, he sat down on the sofa opposite. He watched as she gulped the water down. She drank in silence, determined not to be the first one to speak. But when she slapped the glass down on the coffee table and he still hadn't spoken she'd had about enough of the tension snapping in the air. 'I thought you had something to say. If you don't, I'll go.'

She went to get up, but stopped when he shook his head and held up a hand.

'Don't go, Jess. I…' He stood up, paced to the window and back. He didn't just look nervous, she realised as he sat back down. He looked scared.

'I have stuff I need to tell you. But it's stuff I never told anyone before and I don't know how to say it.' He sounded like an idiot, Monroe thought grimly. 'I wanted to explain, about what happened. You know, when you told me about the baby. Why I lost it.'

'You already explained that, Monroe.' Her voice was curt, dismissive. Frightening him even more.

'No, I didn't, not properly.'

Her eyes widened, but she didn't reply.

He wanted to touch her, to pull her into his arms and bury his face in her hair. He wanted to make the horrible memory of what he'd said and done just go away. But he knew he couldn't. Seeing the anguish in her eyes only made him remember the ugly scene more clearly. She was probably remembering it, too. He had to make it right, even if it meant exposing himself to the kind of heartache he'd struggled so hard his whole life to avoid.

No way could he look at her while he did it, though. He walked back over to the window, plunging his fists deep into his pockets.

'Before you told me you were pregnant, I'd already decided I had to let you go. And it was killing me.'

'What do you mean, you'd decided?' He could hear the anger in her voice. 'But I thought you…'

Monroe swung round, but she'd gone silent, and very still. Beneath the bright light of temper in her eyes, Monroe could see the dark flush of embarrassment, humiliation.

The guilt swamped him.

She'd opened herself up to him, had been honest and forthright about her feelings, while he'd been secretive and cowardly, hoarding his emotions like a miser scared to let go of his loot.

He forced himself to walk back across the room, sit beside her. She straightened, but didn't move away.

'Jess, I can't keep saying I'm sorry. What I want to do is tell you the truth.' He reached for her hands, held on when she tried to tug them out of his grasp.

'You said you wouldn't touch me. You promised.' Her voice quivered.

He stroked the limp palms with his thumbs and looked into her eyes. 'Don't cry, Red. I can't stand it.'

'I'm not crying.' She sniffed as the first tear fell.

'I love you so much, Red.' There, at last, he'd said it.

'What?' She pulled her hands out of his, brushed at her eyes.

'It scared me to death,' he said. 'That's why I let you say it and I never said it back.'

'You can't say this now, Monroe. I won't let you.' He had to admire the steel in her eyes. 'I don't believe you.'

He touched his forehead to hers briefly. 'I know you don't, Jess. And I don't blame you. But it's the truth, I swear.'

Somehow Jessie found the strength to stand up, to step away from him. 'If you loved me you never would have said those things to me.' Her voice hitched. How dared he tell her this now, when it was too late? 'If you loved me, Monroe, why did you never ever say it to me?' Just thinking about how he had rejected her in so many subtle ways brought the anger back. 'I told you how I felt and I waited like an idiot for you to say it back, but you never did.

It was always, "Sure, baby," or, "That's nice," or some other lame response. You made my feelings seem silly and immature.'

He stood up. She took another step back.

'I didn't say it because I couldn't,' he said quietly.

'Why couldn't you?' She could feel the tears running down her cheeks now, but she didn't stop to brush them away. Why should she feel ashamed of them?

'Jess, no one had ever loved me before the way you did. My mother hated my guts, Linc cared about me, but there was always so much guilt and responsibility between us. No woman I'd ever slept with had meant much more to me than a good lay. I treated them nice when I was with them, but I never missed them when I moved on. With you, right from the start, it was different. The way you turned me on. The way you responded to me. Your honesty, your openness. You never held anything back. You told me you loved me and I was…' he paused '…I was stunned. I knew I didn't deserve you and knowing I couldn't keep you was destroying me. If I'd have told you how I felt, it would have just made it harder to let you go.'

'If you couldn't tell me you loved me—if you knew there was no future—why did you still make love to me?'

He stopped dead, and his faced flushed.

'Every time we made love, Monroe, you were pulling me in deeper. You must have known that.'

'I did, I guess. I figured it was something I could give you back.'

Could it get any more humiliating than this? she thought. 'So now you're saying I was some kind of mercy lay.'

'Jess.' He tried to grab her arm but she spun away. 'I couldn't keep my hands off you. You weren't a mercy lay, it was the best sex I'd ever had in my life. When I figured out the reason why, that I was in love with you, it only made it worse. Because I knew it was going to hurt us both when I had to let you go.'

Jessie frowned. 'Why do you keep saying that? Why would you have to let me go? What are you talking about?'

His face was rigid with frustration. 'Isn't it obvious? What the hell could I offer you? I was an ex-con, no fixed abode. Living off my brother's charity like some damn deadbeat. Your dream is to have kids, a family, a home. All I could give you was good sex.'

'Whoa! Hang on just a minute.' She held up her hand. He actually believed what he was saying, she could see it in his eyes, beneath the anger, the frustration. 'You're serious about this?'

He sank his fists back into his pockets, his voice sharp and annoyed. 'Of course I am.'

She couldn't believe it. He'd rejected her, had put them both through hell, had even convinced himself the baby wasn't his, out of some twisted sense of gallantry.

He really did love her. She could see it behind the temper and embarrassment. She felt the heavy, dragging weight that had been lodged in her chest for days begin to lift.

Her lips quirked, relief warring with disbelief.

His eyes darkened. 'What's so funny?'

'You are, Monroe. You mean to say that because you went to prison all those years ago you thought you weren't good enough for me?'

'Well, yeah.' It suddenly sounded dumb to Monroe, too.

She stepped up to him, placed warm hands on his cheeks. 'Monroe, you complete fool.'

Annoyed or not, humiliated or not, he wasn't going to miss the opportunity to touch her at last. He put his hands on her hips and pulled her closer. 'So, do you believe that I love you now?'

She smiled into his eyes, but only said, 'Hmm.' He went to wrap his arms around her, but she slipped away, leaving him empty-handed again.

She pointed a finger at him when he tried to follow her. 'Don't come any closer, Monroe,' she said. 'I want to get something straight here.'

Monroe didn't like that considering look in her eyes, or the fact that she'd been close enough to smell and now she was gone again.

'So you mean to tell me *you* decided you weren't good enough for me?' she said.

'Yeah, that's right.' He wasn't sure where this was leading, but he had a feeling he wasn't going to like it.

'And *you* also decided that you were going to let me go.'

He nodded, warily.

'And then, when I told you I was pregnant, you panicked. You accused me of cheating because—' she paused for effect '—let's face it, it was easier to jump to that conclusion than to have to actually deal with all those messy emotions that you didn't want to deal with.'

At this point, he decided, it was probably best to keep his mouth shut.

Jessie walked up to him and poked him hard in the chest. He stumbled back, shocked to see the satisfaction in her face when he did.

'And, although when you thought about it you knew I hadn't slept with someone else,' she continued, the glint of steel in her eyes making him very nervous, 'it still took Linc to persuade you to go and get checked out.'

'Okay, so I was an idiot.' What the hell else did she want from him?

'You weren't just an idiot, Monroe. You were a coward.'

He bristled, but looked her square in the eyes and nodded. 'Yeah. I was.' He took her arm in a firm grip and pulled her back to him. The tantalising scent of summer flowers made him ache. 'Jess, just tell me, do you still love me, despite all that?' He couldn't wait any longer to know for sure.

She stared at him for a long time. 'You know, I'm not sure if it was really love in the first place.'

It seemed a lifetime ago, Jessie thought as she watched Monroe's face fall.

The eager, impulsive, stupidly romantic girl she'd been but a week before was gone. In her place was a woman, with a woman's heart, a woman's love and a new life growing inside her.

He dropped her arm. He looked bewildered and hurt, but Jessie knew she had to see this through, for both of them. She hadn't been fair to him, either. She could see that now. She'd put him on a pedestal, when he was just a man—a man who'd been through hell and had all the insecurities to show for it. She hadn't seen him for what he was. Funny, now she did, she loved him so much more.

'I idolised you,' she said, thinking back. 'You were gorgeous, cooler than cool with that Harley and that easy, devil-may-care

charm. And you were incredible in bed. You gave me an orgasm.'
The heat throbbed low in her belly at the memory.

'Hey, I gave you a lot more than just one,' he said—rather testily, she thought.

'But it wasn't really love. It was infatuation. I can see that now.'

'Well, thanks a bunch.' He sounded angry but she could see the pain in his eyes. 'I've bared my damn soul and now you're telling me you don't love me.'

'Now, now, don't get all surly.' It was cruel to tease him, but she couldn't help it. Maybe she wanted him to suffer, just a little bit. 'Even though it suits you.'

'What, you think this is funny?' Okay, so he was shooting past surly straight to furious.

'No, what I'm saying is, I didn't love you then, because I didn't know you. You were some ridiculous white knight, to me. A romantic dream I could never have. Of course, that all came tumbling down when you told me you thought I'd cheated on you.'

He groaned. 'Please, can we forget about that?' He slid his hands round her waist, looked relieved when she didn't pull away.

'I'm sorry, Monroe, but that one's going to get thrown at you every time we have a row. And I'm telling you now that every time it does I'm going to love you more.'

His eyes flared with hope. 'What did you say?'

'I said, I'll love you even more, Monroe.' She ran her hands up his back, felt the tension ease out of his shoulders. 'Because I'll know that you're not a white knight, or some super cool dude who's too damn gorgeous for me. I'll know that you're really surly and unsure of yourself and, like most men, don't know a damn thing about how to express your feelings. You've got just as many hang-ups—actually you've got a lot more hang-ups than I have. And a chip on your shoulder the size of a Californian redwood.'

'Hold on a minute.'

She grabbed hold of his hair and kissed him hard on the lips before he could say anything else.

'But you know what?' she said.

'What?' He looked really confused now.

Jessie felt the love inside her swell to impossible proportions.

'You're mine. With all your problems and daft ideas about yourself. We're going to have this baby and it's going to be loved and cherished by both of us and when it drives us nuts—and it will—we'll know how to deal with it. Because we learnt the hard way, having to deal with each other.'

'You think?' The cocksure grin she knew so well spread across his face, making her blood heat. 'So, let me get this straight,' he said. 'You're saying you do love me, now?'

'Uh-huh.'

'No, I don't think so.' He hugged her tight, lifted her off the ground. 'Uh-huh won't do it. You've got to say it.'

'Oh, all right, if you insist.' She wanted to sound miffed, but the lilt in her voice, the joy leaping in her breast, made it impossible. 'But only if I get another orgasm—and soon.'

'You got it.' He grinned, put strong hands on her butt and pulled her against him so she could feel the hot, hard length of his arousal through his jeans. 'Now say it, Red.'

'I love you to bits, you big oaf.'

'Okay, that's it.' He swung her up into his arms, and strode across the room heading for the bedroom door with her high in his arms. 'One orgasm coming right up.'

She laughed, clung onto his neck and covered his lips with hers.

EPILOGUE

'WILL you sit down? You're nearly six months pregnant, woman.'

'My point exactly, darling. I'm pregnant, not an invalid.' Jessie grinned at Monroe's annoyed expression. 'I think the hormones must be messing with my brain cells. But I'm actually finding that Lord and Master routine of yours quite a turn on.'

Monroe put his hands around her waist, caressed the soft swell of her belly. Arousal dimmed the annoyance in his eyes. 'I'm warning you, Mrs Latimer.' He pulled her to him, dropped his voice to a whisper. 'If you don't do as you're told, you're gonna pay.'

Jessie wedged her hands against his chest. 'Don't you dare kiss me here, Monroe. It'll end up in the morning papers.'

She peered over his shoulder at the beautiful people that thronged around them, resplendent in their Christmas finery. The clink of champagne glasses and animated conversation, mostly being conducted in loud New York accents, echoed off the art gallery's bare brick walls. Even though they were discreetly tucked away in a corner, she could see their little embrace had already attracted attention.

She eased Monroe back. 'Stop pestering me and go and do some more schmoozing. You're the star attraction tonight, remember.'

It was the opening of Monroe's second show at Carole Jackson's elegant New York gallery. Even on Christmas Eve, with the traffic a misery outside and the weather even worse, the space was crammed with the art world's movers and shakers.

Monroe gave a frustrated sigh. He kept his arm around her waist as he turned to survey the crowd. 'I guess I can give it another twenty minutes. But that's it. I hate these things.'

Jessie smiled. Four months as the darling of the Manhattan art scene and Monroe Latimer was still embarrassed by his own success.

She could still remember that first dizzying showing when she'd still been plagued by morning sickness and had been sporting a shiny new ring on her wedding finger.

Carole Jackson had got the press salivating beforehand, by feeding them stories about the handsome bad boy who was about to conquer New York. How Monroe had hated that. But over the next month, with his face plastered over every art magazine in the country, even Monroe had to admit that some of the agony had been worth it.

Since then his painting and his celebrity had gone through the stratosphere. His work was hanging in the homes of Hollywood stars, European princes and even on the walls of the White House. Only the day before, they'd been out doing some last-minute Christmas shopping at Bloomingdales and Monroe had been asked for his autograph three times. He'd cringed with embarrassment every time.

'I'm afraid it's all part of the package, honey,' Jessie said, the pride in her voice helping it rise above the noise of the chattering crowd.

Monroe gave her waist a quick squeeze. 'Okay, I'll go butter them up some more, but only if you promise to get off your feet for ten minutes.'

'Stop being such an old woman,' she said mutinously. 'I feel fine.'

He lifted his head. 'There's Linc and Ali. Great—they can keep an eye on you.'

Jessie followed his gaze to see her sister and brother-in-law weaving their way towards them.

Easy kisses and warm greetings were exchanged. Linc got to Jessie first, giving her a kiss on the cheek. 'Jess, you look gorgeous. How are you feeling?'

Jessie patted her protruding stomach, which was prominently displayed in the strapless velvet evening dress she was wearing. 'Wonderful. Now if you could just explain that to your brother.'

'She's been on her feet all day,' Monroe grumbled. 'What with her job at Cullen's and now this.' Monroe shot Jessie an exasperated look. 'She needs to sit down.'

'For goodness' sake, Monroe,' Jessie replied. 'I'm perfectly healthy. I feel absolutely fine. Will you stop obsessing about it?'

Jessie would have said more, but Linc slung an arm around Monroe's shoulder. 'Come on, little brother. Let's go get a beer, and I'll explain the fine art of how not to annoy a pregnant lady.' Winking at Jessie, he drew Monroe away.

Jessie watched as the two men pushed their way to the bar, Monroe fending off the throng of reporters, dignitaries and art lovers who kept trying to waylay him.

'I love the way Linc says that as if he's some kind of expert.' Ali threaded her arm through Jessie's. 'He never stopped trying to wrap me in cotton wool during both my pregnancies.'

Jessie grinned; she could just imagine. 'Well, Monroe needs any help he can get. He's still moaning on about how I don't need to work and why don't I give up the job at Cullen's now that he's doing so well. I think he expects me to sit at home all day and stare at the ceiling. Just to be on the safe side.'

Ali laughed, then rubbed her hand over Jessie's bump. 'It's only because he's completely besotted with you—and the baby. I think it's sweet.'

Searching the room for Monroe, Jessie smiled when she spotted him, looking gorgeous and irritated as a reporter gesticulated madly in front of him.

'You got your dream, then, Jessie?' Ali said quietly beside her.

Jessie thought back to the summer and all the dreams she'd spun when she'd first fallen in love with Monroe.

'Not exactly,' she said eventually. 'My dreams didn't include stretch marks, or enormous boobs.' Ali started to laugh. 'Or puking my guts up for three months solid.'

Ali wiped a tear of mirth from her cheek. 'I'll bet Monroe hasn't complained about the boobs once.'

Both sisters laughed.

It was another hour before Monroe managed to muscle Jessie towards the gallery's front doors. As he grabbed his wife's coat from the hat-check girl, he was feeling agitated, annoyed and more than a little sexually frustrated. He'd been trying to figure out all evening how that sexy dress stayed up.

He grinned as he held the door open for his wife. The surprise he had planned should get things rolling in the right direction at last. Not too much longer to wait before he got his answer.

A cold blast of winter air hit Monroe as he stepped through the gallery's stately glass doors. He tucked Jessie's coat around her shoulders, grabbed her hand and pulled her out onto the sidewalk. Cab horns blasted and the frigid wind whipped down the street, stirring the grey sludge that had been pristine white snow only that morning. Emmy would be thrilled, he thought, if they got snow in Long Island for Christmas Day.

He was relieved to see the long, sedate black limo waiting at the kerb for them. The chauffeur jumped out and rushed round to open the back door, blowing his hands to warm them.

Jessie's teeth chattered beside him. 'It's freezing.' She looked confused as he took her hand and pulled her towards the open door of the limo. 'What are you doing, Monroe?'

'We're not going home tonight,' Monroe said. He could see she was about to protest, so he lifted her up in his arms. 'I've got an early Christmas present for you, Red.'

Jessie clung onto his neck. 'Put me down, you mad man. You'll fall on your bum. The pavement's covered in ice.'

He carried her into the luxurious interior of the limo without a single slip.

'How long are you going to live in Manhattan, sweetheart, before you realise we don't have pavements here, we have sidewalks?' He settled her onto his lap as the chauffeur slammed the door.

'What on earth is this all about, Monroe?' she said eventually.

'Nothing,' he said, wrapping his arms around her waist. 'Just taking my wife out on a date.' He loved the sound of those words; 'my wife.' He still hadn't gotten out of the habit of saying them as often as was humanly possible.

He leaned across and pressed a small button on the console in the door.

The chauffeur's black screen slid back. 'Yes, sir?'

'Take us to the Waldorf, buddy. But we don't want to get there for at least an hour. And keep the screen closed.'

'No problem, sir,' the man replied.

The screen slid silently shut and the car pulled out. The colourful lights and chaotic sounds that were Manhattan at Christmas whirled past outside as Monroe settled into the warm, seductive darkness. The smell of leather and his wife's perfume filled the air. The familiar flowery scent never failed to make his blood heat. He stroked his hands up the soft velvet that clung to her curves. She shivered as he kissed the sensitive skin at her nape. It was incredible the way she responded to him.

Their tongues danced in a well-remembered rhythm. His demanding, insistent, hers giving, seeking, until they were both panting.

Finally, he lifted his head. His deep blue eyes were dark with desire and intent on hers as he twisted her in his lap.

Fisting his hands in her hair, he brought his lips to hers. When they were a whisper apart, he paused, grinned. 'You know, Red. I may never have been your dream guy. But you sure are my dream girl.'

To hell with the dream guy, Jessie thought as she sank into the hot, passionate kiss, the heat throbbing in her core at the promise of what was to come. The real one's much better.

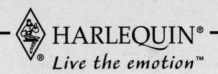
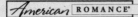

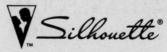

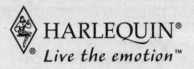

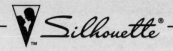

SPECIAL EDITION™

Emotional, compelling stories that capture the intensity of living, loving and creating a family in today's world.

Silhouette® Desire

Modern, passionate reads that are powerful and provocative.

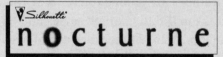

nocturne

Dramatic and sensual tales of paranormal romance.

Romantic SUSPENSE

Romances that are sparked by danger and fueled by passion.

HARLEQUIN®

SuperRomance®

…there's more to the story!

Superromance.
A *big* satisfying read about unforgettable
characters. Each month we offer *six* very different
stories that range from family drama to adventure
and mystery, from highly emotional stories to
romantic comedies—and much more! Stories
about people you'll believe in and care about.
Stories too compelling to put down….

Our authors are among today's *best* romance
writers. You'll find familiar names and talented
newcomers. Many of them are award winners—
and you'll see why!

If you want the biggest and best
in romance fiction, you'll get it
from Superromance!

Exciting, Emotional, Unexpected…

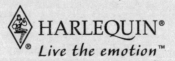

HARLEQUIN®
Live the emotion™

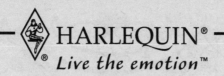

Harlequin® Historical
Historical Romantic Adventure!

Imagine a time of chivalrous knights and unconventional ladies, roguish rakes and impetuous heiresses, rugged cowboys and spirited frontierswomen—these rich and vivid tales will capture your imagination!

Harlequin Historical . . . they're too good to miss!